# Just.Another.Common.Killer

### By: Chantal Bellehumeur

RoseDog✦Books

PITTSBURGH, PENNSYLVANIA 15222

ISBN: 978-1-4349-9932-0
Printed in the United States of America

*First Printing*

For more information or to order additional books, please contact:
RoseDog Books
701 Smithfield Street
Pittsburgh, Pennsylvania 15222
U.S.A.
1-800-834-1803
*www.rosedogbookstore.com*

## I would like to thank the following people:

My close friend, **Matthew Gulliver**, for coming up with the signature notes idea and technically the titles of this book. Our conversation about Jack being short for «just another common killer» got me started on this novel. Thanks for letting me use part of your twisted mind for my modern character. Now, please use it for the greater good!!!

My best friend, **Sarah Wong**, for going on the Jack the Ripper tour with me in London despite the cold and pouring rain, and for continuing to walk around the Whitechapel area unguided afterwards. Thank you for humouring me by going to the 10 Bell's pub. Thanks for giving me my first Jack the Ripper book, which became helpful when I decided to write this novel. It gave me enough basic background information to make the more reality-based part of my outline. Thanks for continuing to keep me updated on the latest Jack the ripper news. It really pushed me to finish my novel after I had put it aside.

I think I should also thank you for accepting to go to the more morbid attractions of London when I was visiting, and for keeping your patience when I felt the need to take pictures of old cemeteries, scenes set up in the London Dungeon as well as the clink museum and practically every door, wall, ceiling and corner of the tower on London. (By the way, there is a man at your window!)

My eight year old son, **Aidan O'Brien**, for contributing his drawing of Jack the Ripper for my novel.

Everyone (especially Matty) who, intentionally or not, provided me with killer bits of inspiration.

My sister, **Karyne Bellehumeur** and Matty (again!) for always answering my random questions when I called during or after writing frenzies, and for listening to me go on and on about the progress of my novel.

My good friend, **Sven Radtke**, for being my German translator.

My neighbours and good friends, **Mike Cole** and **Wendy Farmer**, for letting me use their internet.

My **family and friends** for encouraging me to write, and for not locking me up in a mental institution.

Last but not least, my close friend **Kendal Madill** for taking the time to proof read my manuscript and correct all my spelling and grammatical mistakes. This novel would have been a complete embarrassment without your involvement.

# Acknowledgments:

(Do not read before novel-spoiler ahead!)

Dear readers,

According to my mother, I have always been very creative and inventive.

I remember my younger sister telling the most original tales as a child, trying to make us all believe they were real. I used to make things up as well, but mainly liked to act my stories out rather than verbalizing them. I liked to pretend that I was this character or another, and even demanded that I be called Meagan at one point because I had decided that I was part of the «My Little Pony» entourage. I refused to be called by my real name and would not respond to Chantal. My mother let me go to my Kindergarten class with a star sticker on the side of my eye because I wanted to be Rainbow Bright that day. Those were my cute girly days. For some reason, my ideas and interests turned darker over the years.

Since I learned how to read and write, I enjoyed coming up with multiple stories. I made mini-books, which my parents kept. I felt very nostalgic when my dad gave me my box full of old childhood literature.

I think my sister and I were probably the only children who would make up a basic outline of our games when we played dolls, Barbies or anything in which we became characters. We would both decide whom each person was and what their story would be. Thinking back, our friends must have thought we were really odd. They all preferred to just make up the games as we played, sort of like improvising. My sister and I sometimes had titled for our games so we could reference them.

As I grew older, I started writing longer stories. I still have the short story I wrote about a haunted museum, inspired by the fact that the nature museum in Ottawa was supposedly haunted. I also kept the novel I tried to write when I was twelve, about the ghost of a little girl who haunted her home. I had become really involved in that one!

When my sister and I still shared a bedroom, I pretended that an elf came by to visit my sibling by disguising my voice and speaking to her. She would talk back and ask me questions about the North Pole and Santa. We had full conversations, right after night. I eventually made up other elves and made different voices for all of them. I wondered if my sister actually believed that elves were really there, or if she knew that it was me speaking and just humoured me. Years later, my sister confessed that she was half convinced the elves were

V

real, but eventually figured out that it was me. She looked forward to talking to them anyways because she was entertained, so she played my game.

My sister and I started working on a script together for fun. As we amused ourselves writing our horror movie, «Ouija», we figured out our cast and planned on using our uncle's video camera to make our film. Unfortunately, we never finished the script. We gave up when we realised that it would be impossible for us to do all the special effects we wanted; like having a secret passage open up from the fireplace or having me (the ghost) float and look transparent. I found a copy of our work years later, so kept it aside until my sister could come down to visit me in Montreal. We read what we wrote and had a good laugh. The idea was good but... We both burst out laughing now when we hear the lyrics «I've got the feeling, somebody's watching me» because we had planned on using it in our little movie. Good times!

I moved on to taking theatre classes and forcing my beloved sibling to help me practice Shakespeare lines when I had oral presentations to do in my English classes. I will never forget my father coming up the stairs and telling me to keep my voice down because he could hear me yelling in fits of tears (As Juliet found out that she was being forced to marry Paris the morning after her secret marriage to Romeo.) all the way from the first floor even though he had his office door closed and the door to my sister's room, located on the third floor, was also shut. I got a perfect note though! That's when I started taking acting more seriously.

I was only suited for dramatic roles though, because my voice does not carry out into the audience. I had fun performing in various productions anyways. I loved the rush the shows brought and kept my programs, newspaper articles and ads as souvenirs. When I started working as an extra in the movie industry, I really started missing the stage. But, when my son was born I had less and less time for hobbies outside the home.

I picked up painting and drawing as a hobby, but never considered myself an artist because I have never been able to come up with my own artistic ideas. Unless I do abstract art, I can only copy what I see.

When my son was awake, I put on puppet shows for him, invented little tunes and sang Broadway musicals to him before he went to bed. «Castle on a Cloud» was his favourite. That turned into protective lyrics from Sweeney Todd; «Nothing's gonna harm you. Not while I'm around». Occasionally, I would sing the Phantom of the Opera theme song. Aidan would say: «sing, my angel, sing!», and I would try to vocal out the music as Christine did.

I took singing lessons when I was younger, but never felt that it was for me. The same went for piano, which my parents signed me up for, and guitar, which was part of my junior high school music programme.

At the age of nine, I loved ballet and it was a thrill to perform during my first and only recital, but I quit when our move from Toronto to Ottawa enabled me to perform in «The Nutcracker». I remember being really upset at the time. I took up dance again later on, when I was in high school, and did more shows. But, nothing ever compared to acting.

In high school, I was forced to write poems for class, but composed some on my own as well. I read over them recently. Although I would never publish them because they are way too personal and highly depressing, I found some of them quite good (If I may say so myself). Browsing though everything I had written made me realise how much I had always loved writing. I never considered it as a part time career until I realised that it was very similar to acting, but more feasible as a single mom.

Among my pile of old stories and poems, I found two short stories that I had written for fun but never let anyone, including my significant other at the time, read. «Baby Dolls» was written in 2004, and «Breathless» was written in 2005. I recently re-polished them for possible future publishing.

In 2009, I wrote a novel just for fun and ended up publishing «Veronica's Soap Opera Life». That encouraged me to continue writing so I worked on the sequel to my first novel, «Veronica's Attempt at Romance». Needless to say, my writing style was different than usual, but I went back to writing more suspense.

Since I found out the tale of Jack the Ripper, I have been fascinated by his mystery. As my ex put it, Jack was my favourite serial killer. I was never an obsessed fan of the mystery, but liked his tale enough to go on a Jack the Ripper walk when I was in London and want to know more about the Whitechapel murders. I never did any massive research about the unsolved murder case until I found myself wanting to base a character on Jack. After writing a short first draft, I was rather freaked out to find out the suspect I blindly chose to mostly base my story on is most likely Jack the Ripper according to more recent studies. The fact that Walter Sickert is a lot like me in terms of hobbies scared me a lot. I own several costumes and have a tendency to write extra long letters to friends and family. Hummm. I also really like the story of Dr. Jekyll and Mr. Hyde. But, don't worry! Even if I always felt like I had lived in London in a past life, I don't think I was Jack the Ripper. I am obsessed with Halloween and love horror movies, but would never hurt a fly (Only spiders. Ha,ha) My nickname was Psycho in high school but that was mostly because I liked to scare people.

I love the dark to the point of forgetting to turn on lights sometimes, and barely anything frightens me. The only thing I can think of, aside from the disgusting eight legged creepy crawlers, is the theme song from Unsolved Mysteries. I don't know why, but I can't listen to it without completely freaking out and getting chills. Ok, I have a thing for eyes being touched too. I can watch fake gory scenes, but can't watch my sister put on her contact lenses. Go figure!

I would just like to remind you that this is a fictional novel. So, some of my reality based material is not 100% accurate.

I did end up writing things and ended up finding out that they were facts, which creeped me out again and made people laugh and tell me I had to have lived during the Ripper murders, but I also modified some things to suit my story.

I hope you all liked this book! Sweet dreams!
(Sorry to those I already gave nightmares to!!!)

Yours truly,
Chantal

# Introduction:

(London, England-1988)

Jacqueline Huntington was woken up in the middle of the night by her six year old son's diabolical laugh.

As she walked along the narrow hallway towards his voice, she heard him whispering incomprehensible words and was startled by his sudden echoing shout.

It was not unusual to find Jack sleepwalking at random hours of the night. On several occasions, he had silently mutilated his sister's dolls by either removing parts of their fluffy white stuffing from a tear he had made on the so-called stomachs with the blade of a kitchen knife or cutting off plastic body parts with the same sharp cutlery. Pretty porcelain girls were smashed and left in dozens of pieces around the old Victorian house.

Jack could never remember his psychotic actions in the morning. All his memory would summon were the names he had chosen for the dolls he broke; Emma, Martha, Polly, Annie, Mary, Miss Farmer, Rose, Miss Jackson, Alice and Lydia. He once pointed towards new dolls and called them Francis and Carrie. This was right after pointing his left bony index finger at his younger sisters and verbalizing their names, Elizabeth and Catherine, which he had proudly chosen himself on the days of their births.

Jack was a very sweet boy when he was awake, so nobody understood why he acted out such horrors in his sleep. He was not allowed to watch scary shows, including any cartoons that had monsters, ghosts, mummies, zombies, vampires, werewolves or other creepy characters in them. Books of the same type were not permitted either. Childish war games that included imaginary weapons were frowned upon and Jack always respected the non-violence rule.

When Mrs. Huntington entered her beloved son's bedroom on the rainy night of September 30th, she saw that he was holding his father's silver dissection knife in his right hand. Jack had always given the impression that he was left-handed. The rest of Dr. Huntington's old dissection tools were still in the hard metal case beside him.

Jack's three year old sister, Catherine, lay lifeless right in front of him. Her throat had been cut open, leaving a thin horizontal red line from left to right. The young girl's stomach had been sliced open vertically and torn open on each side. It appeared that some of her internal organs were by her side, in a light pool of blood.

A piece of the dead girl's pinkish nightgown was left a few feet away. On the painted blue wall above the bloody torn fabric, the words "The Juwes are The Men That Will not be Blamed for nothing" were written in powdery white chalk.

It took a few seconds for Mrs. Huntington to understand that she was not having a terrible nightmare. As Jacqueline's shaking right hand rose towards her mouth to hide the hint of a squeal, Jack's head slowly turned towards his mother. "You're next", he told her in his sleep.

Shortly after Mrs. Huntington's discovery, her husband came home from his surgical job at the general hospital to find his five-year-old daughter Elizabeth dead on the kitchen floor.

Her throat had been cut from the right side to the left. Unlike her sister, the rest of her body remained untouched.

Although the experienced doctor was used to seeing open wounds and massive quantities of blood on a daily basis, he became sick at the sight of the darkened ceramic tiles and of his precious daughter's small murdered body. Her blank staring eyes seamed to tell him that he was too late to save her. Nothing could bring her back.

Dr. Huntington discretely dialled the emergency phone number, 9-9-9, before searching his house for the rest of his family. He was careful and silent, keeping in mind that the killer might still be inside his home.

As he walked up the stairs, he saw the moving shadow of a short human being trying to bring down a surgical knife into a taller form. The tall shape managed to grab her attacker's wrist before he could hurt her, but could not take away his weapon. The doctor ran to the scene as fast as he could and was shocked to see his own son trying to wiggle his way out of Mrs. Huntington's tight grasp. The boy grunted furiously while his mother remained speechless and in tears.

The worst was yet to come.

Because Jack was too young to be put on trial for murder and assault, he was treated as a juvenile delinquent and placed under tight surveillance in a mental institution. Jack eventually started seeing a psychologist, Dr. George Philips.

Under hypnosis, Jack Huntington recited murderous tales that had occurred in the Whitechapel area of London, England close to one hundred years ago. The details about the locations of the bodies found, the victims' names and appearances as well as the murders themselves were realistically told as though a grown man was speaking.

Since Dr. Philips was a long time Ripperologist, he recognised Jack the Ripper's history within the boy's stories.

Jack described how, On April 3rd 1888, he attacked a drunken Emma Smith on Brick Lane. He confused her by speaking to her, (and to himself) in different voices, making it seem like she had more than one attacker.

Eventually, his older friend joined in the fun.

Jack confessed to stealing all the money Emma made selling her body that night. He robbed her after repeatedly hitting her in the head and cutting her open here and there. His moves were all spontaneous.

He and his companion did not leave Emma for dead. Jack wanted to see her suffer. While his friend headed home, Jack remained in the shadows and observed his victim. Amused by the woman's strength to get herself up and move forward, he followed far behind Emma as they both slowly made their way towards her house.

Jack overheard Emma tell her neighbour friends about how she almost lost an ear to her attackers, and that she had been raped with a foreign object.

The next day, Jack read in the papers that she had bled internally at the hospital. Not much fuss was made about her death though. No big headline or large story about the brutal attack; just a few boring lines about her death.

On the night of August 6th, Jack stabbed a chubby Martha Tabram a total of thirty seven times in the back of her neck, chest and other random parts of her body. He left her at the bottom of a staircase, letting a pool of warm blood form.

Jack was disappointed that not much attention was paid to this murder either. Most newspapers agreed with Jack in the sense that the unfortunate got what she deserved, but Jack wished that more attention to his work had been given.

It took four days to identify the body, but nobody seemed to care that she was dead so not much was written about it. Nobody even realised that Jack had used two weapons to make it look like Martha had more than one attacker. Jack pointed out that his friend had not been present to participate in the fun this time.

Jack later found out that the only suspects in Martha's killing were soldiers, which highly amused Jack since he had worn a soldier costume that night to wander the streets. The suit had been easy to obtain from Angel's Theatrical Costumes that day because of the Duke of Edinburgh's birthday festivities.

Although he had enjoyed the fireworks, concerts, shows and chamber of horror, the highlight of the celebration had been the first successful murder of his life. Knowing that the police were already on the wrong track made him laugh with content. He had obviously been seen with Martha, but his disguise had been perfect. It was because of this night that Jack chose to become other characters when he walked alone in the dark streets.

Mary Ann Polly Nichols was unfortunate to have Jack as a client on the early morning of August 31.

After looking straight into her dark brown eyes and fantasizing about being inside her, he turned Mary Ann around and reached forward to make two quick cuts across her throat.

Jack didn't want to risk getting her possibly infected blood all over him. Being drenched in Martha's questionable blood had been bad enough. He had been completely disgusted once he realised the consequences his actions might involve. Prostitutes carried diseases, and spread them.

When the surprised woman fell to the ground, he placed her on her back and watched as she gurgled her own blood and eventually drowned. As she was dying, Jack ripped up the bottom half of her body.

He left the Nichols woman wide eyed in Buck's row with her skirt up and her new bonnet on the ground.

Jack later returned to the Ten Bells pub, where he had spotted ugly Polly. She had been missing five teeth when he met her, but Jack liked woman whom did not fit the ideal of beauty because it made him feel more superior. He preferred woman that were either disgustingly bony or morbidly obese.

Before going back for some whiskey though, Jack had fun watching Mary Ann's body being taken away from the crime scene in a hand drawn cart. Her blood dripped onto the sidewalk all the way to the private mortuary she was brought to. Jack followed the dry trail the next day and was almost tempted to walk into the death house. Instead, he took a mental picture of it and headed to his study room.

The night of Mary Ann's murder, Jack remained nearby as pails of water were poured onto the ground to make the red liquid that had escaped the prostitute's body run into the nearby gutters. Jack liked to hide in the dark and observe the effects his work had on others.

Eight days later, Jack murdered an overweight, blue eyed and dark haired Annie Chapmen in the backyard of a lodging house on Hanbury Street; 29 Hanbury Street to be exact.

She was missing her two front teeth and wasn't very attractive, even with her mouth closed. Jack cut her throat to the point of almost succeeding in detaching her head from her neck, and had fun mutilating her dead body.

As instructed, Jack cut up a chunk of her stomach and took out her bowels. He placed everything on the ground beside Annie's left shoulder to get the pieces out of his way. Before he could take out her uterus, a presence was heard.

"You could always tell the police were coming because you could hear their heavy boots from far away. They might as well have blown their whistle and shouted that they were nearby!", Jack laughed.

In any case, he had time to rob Annie and left her in the yard with her left hand resting on her left breast and her right arm at her side.

The next day, Jack was amongst the agitated and curious neighbours gathered around the closed yard to see the bloody mess. Annie's body had been taken away by then, but everyone still wanted to pay their way in to look at the scene of the crime.

Jack mailed a postcard confessing that he had Annie's rings in his possession. He had forced them off her chunky fingers. On his letter, he had drawn a cartoon of the dead woman with the words "poor Annie".

Although unwilling, the newspaper's headlines encouraged Jack to strike again.

On September 9th, Jack dismembered the body of a rich woman.

He dumped most of her body pieces in the Thames River. Her right arm was found in the mud, brought in by the tide, on the 11th.

On the 3rd of October, her naked torso was discovered inside a vault, near Whitehall. This was the very spot were Scotland Yard's new building foundation was. The maggot-infested torso was badly decomposed and was missing its genitals as well as its uterus. Jack had buried a left leg a few yards away, but it took a while for it to be dug up.

Taking a slight pause in his story, Jack briefly mentioned that he always carried his razor blade with him along with one of the many long bladed knives he sharpened every day. He sometimes liked to leave one of his bloody knives on a random street to be found. He always chose five inch blades for that. The whole thing was part of his game; commit a murder on one street, and walk a distance to leave the wrapped weapon elsewhere to confuse the police.

He soon started carrying the Kukri knife his friend had given him as a gift. He loved it because the blade was curved and he could easily sever limbs with it.

Jack continued his tale by telling Dr. Philips that he had written a letter to the central news office, using red ink. In the letter, he mentioned that he had saved some blood from his last victim, but that it had gone too dry to write with. While mocking the police in wishing them good luck in finding him, he described his plan to cut his next victim's ears off so that he might send them to the police.

On September 30th, Jack found two victims; blue eyed and dark haired Elizabeth Stride and a thin, brown eyed and long black haired Catherine Eddowes, whom he accidentally mistook for Mary Jane Kelly because the unfortunate often told people her name was Mary Kelly.

Jack was hiding under the window of 40 Berner Street, listening to an intense German debate when he saw Liz walking all by her lonesome self.

He lured her into the deserted yard with Cachous and cut her throat while she had her back turned. Elizabeth brought her hand to her throat before falling to the ground. Jack continued his work.

After hearing hoarse steps coming in his direction, Jack left Elizabeth's cut up body in Dutfield yard, near Berner Street. She was lying on her left side facing the wall and still holding on to the brown paper bag of treats Jack had generously given her. Some of the breath fresheners had spilled on the dirty ground and mixed with small rocks.

Shortly after Jack left the scene, he heard people hysterically yelling, "Murder!" He continued walking for about fifteen minutes and saw Catherine. He surprised her by cutting her throat as well and laid her on her back with her palms facing upwards.

Jack cut through the lower part of her eyelids, mutilated her nose and butchered the right side of her face. He cut off her right ear lobe and hid it inside Catherine's filthy clothes. Jack lifted up her dress and cut up the material so that he could open up her stomach. He tore out her intestines and placed them beside her right shoulder. He took some organs, (a kidney and half a uterus), for his personal use. Afterwards, he stabbed Catherine's genitals and thighs. He planned to dismember both of her legs but did not have the time. He left her disfigured, with her legs spread on the sidewalk of Mitre Square.

Jack walked a few streets away, in the direction of his previous crime location and left a chalked misspelled message on the wall above a piece of Catherine's apron. He had used the now bloody fabric to wipe his hands.

Jack came back to his third attention grabbing location of the night and asked the police what was going on. By that point, the message he had written had been completely erased.

Jack walked by Catherine's crime scene the following day and saw a bloody outline of Catherine's body on the pavement. She was partially identified by her clothing, like many of the others.

The press received a post card from Jack dated October 1. It briefly described his double murder. He apologized for not having the time to cut up the ears for the police. "I am sure somebody found the ear lobe I left behind though", Jack announced. "It most likely rolled out of Catherine's dress when she was being examined in the morgue."

Jack was proud to see a copy of his two letters in the form of a poster, asking people's help to identify the writer. "I told them they could not trace me by my handwriting, so it was no use trying but..." Jack lifted his shoulder in a "what can you do" sort of way.

Jack's most famous letters were published in the newspapers the following day. He kept that day's paper as a souvenir.

He wrote another letter on the 16th of the same month, purposely leaving a long smear of blood on the page. Jack sent half of Catherine's kidney along with it. The parcel with the preserved organ was sent directly to George Lusk, the chairman of the Whitechapel vigilance committee. Jack admitted to eating the other half of the kidney. "It was quite delicious.", he added after licking his lips. Jack mentioned in his letter that he might send Mr. Lusk his bloody knife next time, but he never did. He never intended to. He simply enjoyed playing games and teasing everyone involved in his case. He dared Mr. Lusk to catch him if he could. "Obviously, he never did!", Jack said in a burst of laughter. "Ha, ha!", he finally said.

Jack admitted to writing several teasing letters and even poems, most of which were mailed to police commissioner Charles Warren. He also sent some of his notes and telegrams to Inspector Abberline, who led his investigation, and a fun message to Dr. Openshaw to let him know that he had been right about wanting to take Catherine's left kidney instead of the right one while he operated on her near his hospital.

Jack wrote so many letters during the month of October that he lost count of them all. Some of his letters included stick figures and child like drawings. He always made sure to include several incorrectly spelled words in his messages to insinuate that he was not an educated man, and to modify his handwriting a little bit. All his letters, along with other copycat letters mailed from various parts of London and several different countries, were all published; there were about eighty of them that month. He was highly amused and continued to write from time to time. He loved writing! It became a necessary part of his game.

To add to his fun, Jack sometimes wrote false addresses on the corner of his envelopes, or completely scratched out the ones he wrote out. Those were from his temporary lodgings. He often used stationary with his known address written in the corner, but would tear out that part of the paper before sending out his letter.

Police eventually became far too present for Jack's liking. For this reason, he tried keeping a low profile for a short while. Jack remembered the police disguising themselves as woman and mimicking prostitutes. "They might have been more convincing if they had at least shaved their beards," he laughed. "The police were such fools! When I played a role, I made sure I looked the part."

He mockingly told Dr. Philips that he had purposely passed by officers after killing his victims and was barely noticed. He even spoke to some of them about the murders, acting like a concerned citizen.

His best kill was done on November 9th, inside room number thirteen of Miller's Court lodging house. Jack made sure that Mary Jane Kelly's body would be unrecognisable. She could have been her temporary roommate for all people knew! Maria was never heard from since that night, but Jack was sure that he had killed the right girl this time. Unless Mary Kelly disappeared on her own, she was definitely the woman he happily murdered. The woman had cheerfully stated her name and there could not have been another poser.

Jack left such a bloody mess that his work was compared to that of the devil. Nobody had seen Jack enter or leave the small rented room. Since Mary had lost her key, she had to unlock her door by entering her arms through a small hole in her window. It looked like the killer had broken the filthy glass to enter her home and exited the same way he had managed to come in. In reality, Jack was just another one of Mary Kelly's clients who was brought to her room.

Jack briefly mentioned that Mary Kelly had spread the word that the Duke had secretly married a common Catholic girl named Annie Crook after the woman bore their illegitimate daughter, Alice. Mary had been Alice's nanny and had seen the baby's mother being taken away, so she wanted to blackmail the Royal Family for money.

Technically, Jack's services were no longer required after Mary Kelly was dead, but he loved his work so much that he continued playing the game he started before the Royal Family gave him a reason to play.

Jack felt the need to get rid of as much vermin as possible. He disliked woman very much; especially those who sold their bodies. He disliked those who flaunted their beauty as well, and the men who possessed them. He killed both men and woman outside of London.

After killing Annie Farmer by cutting her throat open eleven days after butchering Mary Jane Kelly, Jack was highly disappointed that not much fuss had been made. People started believing that Jack was done his work and might have left the city for good.

Jack left England to seek new attention. "I wrote to the police to let them know that I was going to make my way to Paris to start my little games. Nobody took me seriously. I killed two women there, but a connection was never made to me.", Jack said. The French papers wrote small articles about the murders, but it did not make citizens panic like those in Whitechapel.

Upon his return, Jack found out that a letter had been sent in his name to warn people that he was going to kill the first youth he saw. He was never able to hurt children though. There was an innocence about them that made him incapable of hurting them. He did not want that part of his personality known so he pretended to be more vicious than he really was. Several boys were murdered during his fame, but not by him. Some copycats wrote about the murders and pretended it was him. Although he would never be able to rip the heart out of a child, he never attempted to deny such acts when letters describing those actions were signed Jack the Ripper.

Less and less letters were published.

Back in Whitechapel, Jack found Rose Mylett on December 20th. After pulling a rope around her neck to strangle her, he left her with her mouth closed in Clarke's yard. He wanted to try something new! The only clue he left the police was a handkerchief; all his victims had scarves or handkerchiefs. He owned a red one that he was very fond of. It was his good luck charm. Nobody, aside from himself, was allowed to touch it at any given point or he would throw a fit.

Jack left the city again, only to return in June.

Elizabeth Jackson was the first woman he killed once he was back in London. He was unable to complete the dismemberment he had planned because he anticipated the arrival of an officer. Although most officers had started wearing boots that made less noise, Jack saw a hint of a twitching yellow-orange light moving towards him and knew it was time to go.

He hid in the shadows to spy, as he often did after his murders. He loved the darkness.

Jack had the chance to dismember several females that month, and dispersed their remains around the city.

He cut Alice McKenzi's throat on the night of July 17 1889, and left her in Castle Alley with her dress up to expose the mutilation he had done to her abdomen.

On September 8, Jack dismembered Lydia. He scattered her body parts all over town.

Before doing so, he dressed up as a soldier and ran up to a newspaper carrier to let him know that there had been another murder. He gave the man the location of where he planned on leaving Lydia's torso and left.

The decomposed torso with its arms still attached was found near Pinchin Street, as Jack had reported. But, this discovery was only made on the 10th.

On the 4th of December, he wrote to the police to let them know that he was going to try disjointing a hand and send them a finger if he managed. On the 19th, part of his victim was found. The little finger of the right hand was missing two joints.

Jack came in and out of the East End of London for almost two years, leaving human bones and body parts here and there. He left a parcel in the garden of a school for the blind. Inside was a female arm.

During one of his travels, Jack stayed at the Lizard hotel in Cornwall and vandalised the guest book. He did random drawings and wrote vulgar comments and poems inside. He signed one the pages by his famous killer name beside the long nose of a man he had drawn, but nobody took notice. He used up a lot of pages for his personal amusement. He even corrected the grammar and spelling of other guests.

In February of 1891, Jack cut another prostitute's throat in Swallow Garden. Her name was Francis Coles. He fled the scene once her body dropped to the ground because he heard light footsteps coming in his direction. Jack was very attentive to his surroundings. The only thing he left behind was a half eaten grape vine, which was unnoticed.

His last Whitechapel victim was Carrie Brown, whom he murdered on April 24 of that same year. But, he was far from being done his work. He continued to dismember females whenever he could until the day he died.

"What a dance I was leading! Didn't I laugh!" Jack said as he finished his story.

At the end of the first hypnosis session, Dr. Philips asked the boy if he knew whom Jack the Ripper was. Still under hypnosis, he responded that it was him.

Dr. Philips got into the habit of asking the boy whom Jack the Ripper was after each session. Jack always looked up at the doctor with a crooked smile and responded, "I am."

Eventually, Dr. Philips started naming suspects (Albert the Duke of Clarence, Dr. William Gull, Dr. Thomas Barnardo, convicted murderer William Bury, previous surgical student and wife -poisoner George Chapment,

Nathan Kaminsy the violent boot maker, dismissed teacher Montague Druitt, woman hater Aaron Kosminski, murderer and diary holder James Maybrick, medically trained Michael Ostrog, prostitute frightener John Pizer-also known as "Leather Apron" , artist and actor Walter Sickert, Mary Jane Kelly's lover Joseph Barnett who wanted her off the streets, Alfred Napier Blanchard-who confessed to the crimes like John Fitzgerald, Benjamin Graham and William Bull did, Dr. T. Neil Cream, brain fever survivor and a lunatic hearing voices from his dead mother, Frederick Deeming, vicious murderer Carl Feigenbaum, witness George Hutchinson, poet Francis Thompson, night wanderer Nicholas Vassily, Dr. John William, physician Francis Tumblety who fit THE typical serial killer profile, homicidal asylum patient David Cohen, writer Lewis Carroll, violent Jewish asylum patient Hyam Hyams who attached patients and medical staff members, insane James Kelly, butcher Jacob Levy, a man of many trades Alois Szemeredy, studious James Kenneth Stephen, Dr. Pedachenko…) and asked Jack if he was this person or another. Each time, Jack would respond: "It's one of the many possibilities."

Since Dr. Philips never believed that all the Whitechapel murders were the work of a single man, he did not care if one suspect or another had eventually been ruled out. He named them all in hopes that Jack Huntington would give out a clue that would lead to the identity of Jack the Ripper or perhaps even the murderer(s) of other victims. A lot of people had pretended to be the famous Ripper in the past.

Dr. Philips went so far as asking Jack questions such as his profession, training, and knowledge. He asked if Jack was connected to the government in any way, if he travelled a lot on business and if he had been convicted of crimes or put away in an asylum. In desperation for an answer, he even asked if Jack had been a woman. However, Jack always responded: "That's an interesting theory", without elaborating any further.

Of course, Dr. Philips knew how crazy it was to believe that the boy's soul was Jack the Ripper reincarnated. He kept that thought to himself, but secretly hoped to discover whom Jack the Ripper was. He did not know what he would do with that information, except maybe publish his new analysis. He simply had a desperate need to push the boy for answers.

Jack only responded something other than one of his usual single sentences on one occasion, but the information he gave was unhelpful to Dr. Philips. The boy added that he was not the Elephant Man despite many ridiculous rumours, but that he had paid to see Merrick's grotesque and deformed body at the carnival.

He had enjoyed seeing the nightmarish man with deformed bones and huge bags of access skin, caused by his cell growth decease, and helped circulate the impossible story that this heavy headed man with an inside out lip walked out of the hospital in the darkness to stalk the only woman who should not turn him down for sex. This monster would supposedly butcher up the unfortunates, dressed in a black hooded cloak. The reasoning behind it was that they refused to let him be their client, no matter how much money he offered them.

Dr. Philips, along with most intelligent people, knew that the sensitive and loving man doomed by his outside appearance could not have possibly been Jack the Ripper. Despite the cruel way he had been treated all his life, this was not a hateful human being in the least. On top of that, he was confined to his hospital room and would not have been able to leave unnoticed.

The driven doctor continued asking his routine questions, but was never given clear details on Jack's personal background.

Jack hinted a few times that he had rather enjoyed the live performance of "Dr. Jekyll and Mr. Hyde" at the Lyceum Theatre, and that it had inspired him greatly. He also liked the violent puppet shows of Punch & Judy. He attended a lot of stage productions, including "Hide and Seekyll" at the Royaly Theatre. He often entered the music hall theatre to seek entertainment.

That is as far as he went into his personality, which gave absolutely nothing away according to Dr. Philips.

Jack teased the psychologist once by telling him that he had never shared the same title as him, but Dr. Philips never got clarification from the boy if he meant the he had never been a psychologist or a doctor. The boy told him he owned a black medical bag, but then said that it might not have been a real doctor's bag.

During one of his hypnotic sessions, Jack was asked to draw a portrait of himself. This is what the young boy drew:

by Aidan O'Brien

As far as the boy's troubled parents were concerned, Jack had never heard of Whitechapel's nineteenth century mystery killer, or anything concerning London's Victorian days. He had obviously never been shown how to cut open a body so cleanly.

Mr. And Mrs. Huntington did not own any history books, or even encyclopaedias. The only books in the house were medical related books, with barely any pictures in them. There were a few pages with anatomy diagrams, but the manuals were on high shelves and could not be reached by the children; even if they stood on chairs.

Jack had never been read a Charles Dickens story, not even at Christmas. He had never seen a Lewis Carroll book. Mrs Huntington and her husband thought both popular authors were too odd. They did not have very creative minds and almost condemned those with wild ideas. Drugs surely had to be involved in the making of the fictitious tales. Dr. Seuss, the American children's book writer, was considered to be a modern weirdo on acid by the Huntington's.

Jack was certainly never told the fictitious tale of Dr. Jekyll and Mr Hyde, although Mrs. Huntington remembered her son pretending to drink something from an empty medicine bottle in his sleep once and saying that the bad tasting liquid was going to turn him into an evil monster.

"He must have been re-enacting a weird episode of Looney-Toons he had seen at his old daycare," Mrs Huntington suggested. She could not control what her son watched when he was being babysat outside the house. She disapproved of silly non-educational shows, saying they were a waste of time.

Mrs. Huntington felt the same about computer games. She was under the impression that looking at a screen for too long might lead to brainwashing. The home computer was barely ever turned on and had no games installed on it.

But Jack's first grade class had one in the corner, and the children could earn good behaviour points to play simple games. Mrs. Huntington thought that subliminal messages might have been inserted into Jack's mind.

Jack could not have been aware of Jack the Ripper's existence. However, Jack was once overheard saying in his sleep that he had given birth to the twentieth century. His handwriting, when using his left hand, matched that of the three notes known with absolute certainty to be written by the original killer in 1888.

His signature, under hypnosis, was too much of a replica to the one on the famous letters to be a coincidence. The boy never signed his real name during the therapy sessions; always Jack the Ripper. It always matched the original killer's. The first letter of the name was never capitalized or had a dot above it. The letters "c" and "k" were always slightly detached from the rest of the word Jack, as was the second "p" and letters "e" and "r" detached from the word Ripper. The dot on the "i" resembled closely to a tiny heart.

# Part 1

## (The growing monster)

# Chapter 1:

Jack Huntington had spent almost four years under the surveillance of Dr. Philips. He was placed under hypnosis so many times, that his once intriguing stories eventually became quite boring and highly monotonous.

Since Jack started giving out less and less information about the Whitechapel murders once Dr. Philips became too persistent about personal details, the doctor grew tired of listening to Jack talking in different languages, mostly German, about events that had occurred before he was even born, and hearing him say that nobody would ever know his true identity despite all the clues he purposely spread around London. "People still look at them today without even realising what they see", he would say. "Everyone is still so blind!"

Dr. Philips' original theory about the boy seemed more and more ridiculous. He began to think that he might have undergone a momentary phase of insanity because of his personal obsession with Jack the Ripper.

He had a large collection of old newspaper articles he found about reported murders in or around Whitechapel between 1888 and 1891. He managed to get his hands on some duplicates of other relevant documents, such as police and autopsy reports that did not end up being destroyed or lost. He paid good money for photocopies, and even a few originals, of over two hundred and fifty letters mailed in Jack the Ripper's name that had been safely stored, old drawings done by various artists reproducing Jack the Ripper scenes and the mysterious man in a top hat, as well as several books enumerating the various theories developed about the numerous suspects and possible victims.

So many suspects had been brought up over the years, and a lot of them had been proven innocent either before or after their deaths. Some of them HAD to be the killer, but intense research eventually proved the impossibility of it. They either did not fit the general Jack the Ripper profile most witnesses had helped portray, had solid alibis, were far from London during some of the murders...Other facts kept suspects on the lists, but with very little to work with in terms of proof.

Like all the theories on each suspect, there had also always been questions concerning how many victims Jack the Ripper really had. There were the famous five; Polly Mary Ann Nichols, Annie Chapman, Elizabeth Stride, Catherine Eddowes and Mary Jane Kelly.

Some people believed that the first two Whitechapel victims of 1888, Emma Smith and Martha Tabram, were Jack the Ripper's amateur work. Many claimed that they were victims randomly chosen by Jack the Ripper as practice for his five carefully selected victims, while others refused to list them as Ripper's work altogether. After all, Emma had mentioned having more than one attacker. Later on, it was proven that two weapons had been used on Martha. So, it was possible that more than one person had stabbed her as well.

Every other victim and body parts found later on were questionable.

Of course, all suspects were based on theories revolving around whom the victims were, which made it difficult to dismiss some of them. Likewise, some victims were pinned as Ripper murders based on the suspects. The mystery has always gone in circles.

Dr. Philips had published a book himself about his own beliefs on the famous murders.

There was a short period of time in his youth where he thought that John Pizer might have been Jack the Ripper. The man fit the public view of Jack the Ripper. Like the majority of witnesses stated, the Ripper was a short man with a dark beard and a moustache, plus he spoke with a foreign accent.

John looked the part, spoke with a non-British accent, and had the bad reputation of scaring prostitutes. The fact that he had been arrested for similar murders in the past was not in his favour. He had access to five inch blades, Jack the Ripper's main weapon, because he was a butcher. John had been given the nickname of "Leather Apron" and a bloody leather apron was found near Annie Chapmen's body.

However, old police reports stated that this perfect suspect had secure alibis and could not be blamed for the Ripper murders. In fact, John Pizer had to be protected from angry citizens when the Ripper murders reached their peak.

After his professional study, Dr. Philips thought that the Queen Victoria's physician, Dr. William Gull, was behind the main gruesome murders. But he had started doubting himself as he listened to his young patient tell his tale.

He realised that his well investigated theory that the doctor had murdered Mary Ann Nichols, Annie Chapmen, Elizabeth Stride, (Catherine Eddowes by mistake) and Mary Jane Kelly to shut them up was being slightly destroyed by a boy who knew nothing about Jack the Ripper in a waking state, and stopped trying to persuade himself that he might learn something new about the unsolved case.

Dr. Philips still held on to the thought that the Ripper case had a conspiracy behind it because Jack the Ripper documents had been very hard to find, but doubted some of his former beliefs now and hated the fact that he didn't have enough information to form a realistic new theory.

At the present time, he was starting to believe that Dr. Gull might have helped Jack the Ripper instead of being him.

It was a known fact that the doctor had placed Annie Crook, a friend of the four main Ripper victims (excluding Catherine Eddowes), in a mental hospital where he had experimented on her. In consequence, the girl lost her memory so could no longer remember that her husband was really the Duke. She became epileptic and eventually went completely insane. She talked nonsense.

But, come to think of it, the doctor would have been much too old and with amnesia coming and going since the year before the murders started, maybe he would not have been capable of committing brutal crimes and disappearing.

Dr. Gull's right hand had been paralysed after his 1887 attack, but Jack was said to be ambidextrous so Dr. Philips never really took that fact to eliminate his most probable suspect.

Any simple citizen could have found out about the Duke's secret marriage and the fact that he had contracted syphilis because Mary Kelly had apparently started spreading the damaging news. It was therefore possible that a murderer unknown to the Royal Family might have been Jack the Ripper, using the rumour as a way to avoid suspicion on himself. One or more killers could have wanted to add the man's work to their own after the deaths of the main victims became popular.

But, Dr. Philips no longer believed that the Whitechapel murders were from different killers, or even possible suicides like some of the later victims were believed to have been. He was now seeing a link between his old youth theory and the one that was shared by many others today.

Dr. Philips almost wished that he had never met the boy and listened to his nonsense. How could he have thought, for even just a minute, that Dr. Gull and Leather Apron might have worked together? It made even less sense than his belief that Jack the Ripper was reborn.

He figured that the boy might have secretly watched a movie based on Jack the Ripper or overheard a documentary on the television, and subconsciously brought up nightmarish visions in his sleep. Dr. Philips was still unsure how the child managed to memorize so much information, especially the exact dates of the murders, and the full names of the victims. But, the mind works in mysterious ways.

Portraits of Jack the Ripper were not uncommon, so it wasn't too unusual that the boy drew a shadowed figured of what appeared to be Jack the Ripper, especially after talking as though he were the man himself.

His handwriting had to be an odd coincidence. Children always wrote in a sloppy fashion! Plus, if the child had viewed information about Jack the Ripper, the signature would most likely have been one of the images seen.

The boy's capability to speak in many foreign languages while he was asleep was curious, but Dr. Philips was sure that there was a perfectly logical explanation for it too. He could not think of one, other than the fact that the boy might have been a linguist in a past life, which made him laugh. He was, after all, trying to discredit the reincarnation theory.

He had always believed in reincarnation, but did not think it possible for someone to remember a past life. In Dr. Philip's mind, a soul lived on and on from one body to the next and never held on to whom they had once been. They simply moved on.

Dr. Philips began some real therapy with the boy.

Little Jack's knowledge of Jack the Ripper and the Whitechapel murders seemed to diminish. Although he did try to attack some of his female inmates in his sleep sometimes, that problem got under control quickly with anti-psychotic medication. His prescription of Perphenazine made him gain a bit of weight, but the important part was that it also made him psychologically better.

Conscious, asleep and under hypnosis, he was eventually able to tell right from wrong. His sleepwalking and creepy dream talks completely stopped. His dose of medication was gradually lowered, and eventually discontinued. He became a normal boy again, with no more signs of having a split personality.

Once Jack turned ten years old, the day of June 6th, Dr. Philips determined that Jack was all right to re-enter the real world. Just to be safe, Dr. Philips recommended that Jack be placed in an orphanage outside the country, where he would have less chances of getting flashbacks of Jack the Ripper's history.

All of Dr. Philips files on Jack Huntington that included Jack the Ripper related notes were destroyed. Although the doctor-patient rule was always respected, he did not want to risk anyone ever seeing his original theories.

Jack was placed in a Canadian orphanage located in the populated city of Montreal, Quebec. Two years later, a good Catholic family with no knowledge of Jack's dark past adopted him.

His name was officially changed to Jack Duff. Mr. and Mrs. Duff welcomed their pre-teen son into their cozy Montreal home, where he became the perfect son in appearance.

# Chapter 2:

Jack became really fascinated with living creatures.

During his first camping trip, he collected all the bugs he could find and watched their movements. He tore the legs off some of the insects when he thought nobody was looking. Sometimes he pulled off antennae. He tore the long bugs, like slimy worms and centipedes, in half. He took the wings off flying bugs. Jack would always put his insects out of their misery after he was done examining them.

In his parents' presence, he would mostly just observe his creepy crawlers and try to figure out how they moved. Mr. and Mrs. Duff had caught him dismembering bugs from time to time, but they considered his behaviour as normal boyish curiosity. Mr. Duff remembered having done the same with his male friends as a child.

When Jack started grade five at his new English elementary school, he was tagged as a science wiz because he wanted to know everything and could grasp more than the teacher intended on showing the class.

Kids made fun of him all the time for his interest in learning and for his good grades, but Jack kept his inner monster to himself. His parents had taught him that violence never solved anything.

When his classmates harassed him for his favourite snacks (Fruit Roll-Ups, yogurt covered jellies, home made chocolate chip cookies…), he would just give it to them. When they cruelly called out names, he ignored them.

He only fought back once, when an older kid in the sixth grade punched him in the arm for no reason at all. Jack threw a violent punch back and was sent to the principal's office.

Mr. and Mrs. Duff defended their son, even though they had not approved of his action. In their opinion, he should have walked away and gone to see an adult. Jack voluntarily apologized to both his parents and to the child he had punched. He promised that this type of behaviour would not happen again, and he meant it. He had no intentions of becoming a troublemaker.

On Thanksgiving Day, Jack had to help his mother with the turkey. Mrs. Duff loved to cook, but she had issues with getting the insides out of the bird, even if they were all taken out previously and just stuffed back inside unattached.

Jack had volunteered to stick his hand inside the defrosted turkey and pull out what was not needed. "It was kind of gross", he admitted to his mother, but he had enjoyed it at the same time.

During the month of October, Jack became excited by a holiday he had never heard about; Halloween.

Kids dressing up in costumes and asking strangers for candies was unreal to him.

Jack asked to dress up as a doctor. Once he realised that Halloween was also about being scared for fun, he wanted to add a monstrous effect to his costume.

His parents mentioned the names Dr. Jekyll and Mr. Hyde, which made the boy's heart fill up with warmth for a reason he could not understand.

Jack liked the story of the determined doctor, whose experience had gone terribly wrong. He asked his parents to tell it to him every single night since they first told him the frightening tale. Of course, he was given the children's version of it. It became his favourite story.

For his first Christmas with the Duff's, Jack was given a miniature dissection kit and a microscope. They thought he might be a bit young to use the tools on his own, but could learn a great deal under supervision.

Jack indeed discovered a lot of things with his gift.

His kit came with a dead bumblebee, so he cut it up and examined the tiny pieces under the microscope. He spent hours trying to find new exciting things to put on his slides and had fun looking at them with a magnified eye. He purposely cut himself one day to get a sample of his own blood. That had fascinated him more than anything.

By the time Valentine's Day came around, all his classmates respected him and several girls had crushes on him.

He received many store-bought valentines and heart shaped candies, which he nicely accepted. In return, he tried to be creative but only managed to freak out the girls he gave special notes too.

On pieces of pink construction paper, Jack had written the words "Thank you!" and his version of "I love you" with a red marker. In the place of the letter "I" was an open eye, complete with eyelashes. Instead of doodling a symmetrical heart shape for the word love like the other children often did, he had drawn an actual beating heart, with the main arteries and tiny veins visible.

The word you was simplified as "u" . Beside his two first drawings, the "u" almost looked like blood spatter.

Easter was not very amusing to Jack at first. The way marketing worked made it too cute.

He did not have an interest for live little bunnies and peeping chickadees. He made the paper flowers and painted eggshells in bright colours to make his mother happy, but was bored with the school's art projects.

Jack enjoyed the milk chocolates and sweet candies he collected during egg hunts, but his real amusement was at church, of all placed.

Until he had been adopted, Jack had only been taught the writings of the Old Testament. His new religion interested him as much as his old forced faith-which is to say, not at all. He usually fought to stay awake during religious ceremonies, but not this time.

They had a re-enactment of Jesus walking to his crucifixion and Jack was focused on the dramatic scenario. He told his parents that he felt really bad for Jesus afterwards, but he actually felt nothing but excitement. He had imagined himself hammering the nails into the Son of God to keep him on the cross.

When he turned eleven, Jack moved on to bigger creatures for his experiments.

He found out that frogs and toads could explode if they came into contact with salt, so he tried it out. He caught a snake and cut it in half to see if it would continue crawling separately like a worm did.

Jack set up mousetraps inside his parents' home and opened the little creatures up when they got caught trying to take a piece of orange cheese. His parents did not like that type of experimentation so much, so he just explored on his own in the woods.

He made mini flipbooks about the animal testing he did and rapidly turned the pages with his thumb to watch the short animations. He never kept his so called art for long because he got bored of them quickly and never intended to show anybody.

With Jack's persistence, he was allowed to watch light horror movies. They were mostly about giant bugs or aliens; very unrealistic shows. His friends would be scared when they spent the night and he played along, pretending to be frightened too.

Halloween became Jack's favourite holiday.

He asked to decorate the exterior as well as the interior of the house on the first of October and annoyed his parents until they finally caved in and said yes. When they went shopping for decorations, he picked gory and scary ones. He wanted to have the best haunted house on the street.

His wish came true that year. Journalists and reporters were at the house filming and taking pictures of the spooky graveyard his father and him had created on the front lawn, along with the ghosts in the dead looking trees.

They also looked at the dozens of illuminated pumpkins Jack and his mother had carved together.

Jack was very proud. He also liked the attention the media had given him. When he saw his face as Frankenstein on the news, he jumped with excitement. His father kept the next day's papers for him so that he could clip out the pictures of the decorated house and articles that were written about it.

Although Jack was not as enthusiastic about putting up the Christmas tree as he was at decorating for Halloween, he still enjoyed going out and picking a pine tree with his family.

He disliked winter and the cold, but saw that the snow made his picture perfect parents smile so he mimicked them.

He hated Christmas carols and the fact that the same songs played over and over again in the stores, in the school hallways and even at home, but he sang along anyways. He even joined the church choir.

Jack lived his nightmare in silence, hoping to be greatly rewarded. He knew full well that Santa Claus did not exist, but his parents were generous when he was good.

Jack continued to do well in school and impressed everyone.

Most of his friends spent their free time playing video games, but Jack never became very interested in pushing buttons for hours without the reward of learning something. He never saw the point in focusing to get high scores in unrealistic fantasy games or wanting to beat anyone's records. He preferred real life.

At the age of twelve, Jack found out that he could look up pictures of dissected animals on the Internet. Mr. And Mrs. Duff did not mind that so much.

He did as many Internet dissections as he could find. His parents encouraged him to explore and were very supportive of his early decision to become a vet. Jack drew what he saw on his parents' computer screen, which did not concern his parents in the least. They did not want him wasting too much printer ink.

Jack's school projects and research were always filled with details and excellent hand drawn pictures. His oral presentations had entertaining qualities to them. He became a bit of a teacher's pet, but nobody made fun of him for it. Instead, they came to him for educational help or advice. Students liked having him on their team for group work.

He still wasn't allowed to watch big slasher movies, but he and his friends viewed them in secret when they played on television late at night.

Jack never had bad dreams.

By the age of thirteen, Jack became more interested in the human body.

He did not waste his time studying girls like most of the other boys his age. Instead, he looked up the functioning of all the human systems.

Many girls were disappointed by Jack's lack of interested in them, but they moved on. His male friends made fun of him for always turning down pretty girls, but he didn't feel like wasting his time chasing stupid females. He started wanting them, but mostly just wanted to hurt them. He kept those fantasies to himself because he knew they were not normal.

Jack was still a well-behaved boy and all his teachers liked him. They all saw great potential in him.

Jack drew some odd pictures of skulls, complete skeletons as well as naked male and female bodies after browsing the net, but his parents saw it with scientific eyes. They compared their son to Leonardo da Vinci's studies of the human anatomy. By this point, Jack had become quite the artist.

His new goal was to become a doctor though. He did not like animals as much as he pretended to. His pet cat, two hamsters and dozens of fish were used as guinea pigs behind the Duff's backs. He longed for human volunteers.

Jack watched documentaries that bored other children of his age and he spent more time studying than playing. His parents had to remind him to hang out with his friends from time to time and encouraged him to get involved in non-educational activities.

To motive him, they bought him a copy of Robert Louis Stevenson's 1886 publication of "The Strange Case of Dr. Jekyll and Mr. Hyde" for his fourteenth birthday. Jack read the novel so many times that the pages of the paperback book became worn and torn before summer ended.

In his French immersion high school, Jack joined the science club. He loved biology and chemistry, but hated physics.

He mostly secluded himself whenever he could and became a bit of a loner.

Girls no longer liked his odd geeky nature and only looked his way because he had the looks of a model now. Image was everything. Some of the girls who had never met Jack started up random conversations with him. Once he began to talk back, girls normally yawned and found excuses to end their conversation. Jack figured it was probably for the best since all he wanted to do was cut their throats to make them stop babbling. He considered most girls to be manipulative heart breakers who played silly games. Although he was eager to play a game of his own, he was in no hurry to find a girlfriend.

Jack played the studious student, but a lot of his free time was spent writing up horror stories instead of doing his homework. His parents had finally given him permission to watch any scary movie he wanted, and he became influenced by them.

Jack also picked up a slight interest for war movies; particularly those about World Wars One and Two. He got an odd sense of nostalgia when he watched them and felt somewhat connected to the dead soldiers he felt the need to draw. He did not feel sad for them, but rather inspired when it came to his more secretive artwork. He admired Hitler in a way, but did not act like a Neo-Nazi or felt the need to draw swastikas everywhere. He never grew to like playing violent video games. He enjoyed live games of paintball because it felt more real. Jack never considered the army as his future, and showed no interest in becoming a cadet like some of his friends. Although the idea of being trained to kill amused him, serving his country and risking his own life took away the fun. He just enjoyed watching war movies for artistic purposes. That phase did not last very long.

Jack gradually became interested in sex, but not in the same way the other boys his age were.

He did not get sexually aroused by a naked female body because of its exposed breasts, ass or vagina, but rather because he saw skin and meat he could cut through. He got excited by the sight of a woman's vulnerability, so the usual pornography magazines did nothing for him. Rape and torture was his thing.

On the rare occasion that Jack made out with girls, he tried to be a gentleman but ended up being much too rough for their liking.

Jack had a vague recollection of spying on his birth father as a child, and watching him tie up his birth mother before violently penetrating her. Of course, back then he did not understand what his father was doing until he tried doing it to him while his mother hypocritically looked away.

His memory soon remembered his father sodomizing him and his innocent sisters on a regular basis while his mother pretended it never happened. In return for her silence, Dr. Huntington gave his wife whatever she wanted in terms of money and material possessions. The children she never planned to have, meant very little to her.

Jack had been taught at an early age that woman were pieces of meat.

His subconscious brought all the nasty images back, and he started having odd dreams.

He saw a young boy who looked nothing like him, but knew that it represented him as a child. The strange boy, wearing clothes that had gone out of style long ago, looked frightened and fearfully spoke in a foreign language. The father figure, wearing a top hat to complete his outdated outfit laughed at the boy, then became severely serious. The boy had to lie down on a single bed. A woman in a nineteenth century style dress showed up with pointy needles and other sharp medical tools. As she came closer to him, Jack woke up sweating.

The following night, he saw the operation the woman was giving him, if you could call it that. The woman was performing unexplainable surgery between his tied down legs. The boy screamed and shouted in the same unrecognisable language heard in the previous dream, while she tried to reassure him in British English that everything was going to be all right. The man that was his father stood by watching, looking unimpressed with his son.

For several nights Jack dreamed of these vaguely familiar characters, having a sense of deja-vu. He would wake up in pain, even though he had been untouched in reality. It was almost like his body was acting out.

The dreams became so constant that upon wakening he was able to write down everything foreign that was being said by the boy; A mixed up repetition of "Nein", "Vater", "Ich flehe dich an", "Bitte", "Halt".

Using the Internet, Jack discovered that the boy in his dream was speaking German. Everything the youngster said were real words that could be translated into English as "No", "father", "I beg you", "Please", and "stop".

Jack was unable to figure out why he was having such horrible dreams, or how his subconscious was able to bring up German.

His adoptive parents confirmed that he had been adopted here in Canada, and that no record showed that the Jack had ever been to Germany. He could not remember learning the language as a child, but there were several gaps in his memory about his past so he eventually left that mystery alone. He didn't think the dream meant anything.

He did watch a lot of German war movies after all. He always had to read the subtitles because he never understood otherwise. Jack figured that he might have retained some of the language without realising it.


As his early years of high school went by, Jack mainly focused on his studies again and continued to dissect dead things instead of trying to figure out silly girls. He had no use for them unless one might volunteer to let him dissect her. There were a lot of stupid females in his grade, but Jack was positive that none of them would willingly let him experiment on them.

One evening, Jack drew a picture of what a live human dissection would look like, but threw it out as quickly as he had drawn it. Jack was not comfortable with the idea of having somebody find the penciled naked body tied up by the arms and legs, with its open stomach and bulging eyes. It would ruin his good image. He was supposed to be the ideal student; the teacher's pet. He was adored, loved and kind hearted.

His first class dissection was a worm, which he found extremely boring. He almost skipped class that day because he knew that it would not be of any interest to him. It turned out to be more fun than expected.

The smell of the formaldehyde stayed in his memory. Every time he would think about dissections, Jack would hallucinate the smell. The memory of the smell made him want to dissect…

Jack asked his science teacher if he could dissect on his own after school, but his request was denied. Specimens were expensive. That was the reason why students had to work in pairs.

He looked it up on the Internet and discovered that he could purchase formaldehyde preserved animals or internal organs and have them sent directly to his home address, but his parents wouldn't allow it. Formaldehyde was intoxicating and should only be used in a well ventilated room.

Wanting to keep his good boy image, Jack pretended to respect everyone's decision. Deep down inside, he desperately craved what he was refused. He would have to be patient.

Jack's next year's class dissection was a pig foetus.

Everyone complained about the smell of the formaldehyde, but Jack still loved it. He opened up his piglet with extreme fascination, not realising that one of his female classmates was throwing up in the class garbage bin.

When he finally noticed the girl had been sick, everyone was occupied trying to comfort her so Jack took the opportunity to wrap up one of the still eyes and pocketed it for later.

Back home, he took out his old childhood dissection scalpel and cut up the swine eye. Jack accidentally dropped the tiny ball he found inside the eye, and was amused to see it bounce on the hardwood floor like a ball.

Jack regretted not having stolen other pig parts for his amusement.

# Chapter 3:

On a chilly autumn night of a full moon, Jack Duff brought his fourteen year old anorexic girlfriend into the middle of the woods of Mount Royal.

After getting her drunk enough to convince her that having sex on the thick carpet of multicoloured dry leaves was a good idea, the fifteen year old boy tore her clothes off and penetrated her violently.

Angela Turquote's pleading requests to slow down only made Jack more violent. As he climaxed into an orgasm, he strangled his victim with his bare hands. His first conscious kill was more enjoyable than losing his virginity.

The preparations had been a bigger thrill though. He had looked forward to this moment for days and found himself rather disappointed that it was already over. Well, almost. He still had the second half of his plan to complete.

Before dissecting Angela with his hunting knife, he carved the letters J.A.C.K on her forehead, leaving a thin line of blood to dry. He then proceeded to cut her open from the bottom of her throat all the way to her pelvic area, and began to pull out her internal organs.

Using his tiny flashlight, Jack examined each bloody piece as though he wanted to understand their purposes. He decided to keep the heart.

Stained with Angela's blood, Jack wrapped the selected muscle into a cloth and dumped it inside a clean plastic container. He put his first trophy in his backpack and headed towards Castor Lake to clean himself up.

Jack was not worried about anyone finding Angela's mutilated body. He knew the woods well enough to figure out that her smell would soon attract wild animals. If her scattered bones were ever found, they would never be able to connect the remains to him anyways.

His bloodstained clothes and bag were tied and bound to a huge heavy rock. Jack walked as far as he could into the lake and threw the big rock into the moving water.

He came back for his bottle of expensive tequila, which he had stolen from his dad's liquor cabinet. Jack was about to dump it into the lake with the rest of the evidence, but reconsidered his plan of action.

If his father found the missing bottle, he would surely question him. Jack realised that he would rather falsely admit to him and Angie taking a few curious sips of the alcohol, than risking the bottle being found with him and Angie's DNA on it near her dead body, regardless of how little the chances were of that happening.

He had to remember to fill the bottle with a bit of water to make up for the four ounces of liquor he had used tonight. His father barely touched the stuff, but why take any chances. He figured his dad would take more notice of missing liquid than his liquor being diluted.

After an unpleasant naked swim, Jack dried himself off with the towel he has previously taken out of his bag, put some fresh clothes on, and headed home with the plastic container in his hands. It wasn't see-through like most of the containers his parents owned, so he did not worry about possibly being seen with it.

Being careful and prepared, Jack had washed his hands thoroughly before pulling out the towel that was in two individual plastic bags. He also washed the outside of the container before tossing everything into the river.

If any drops of blood fell from him between the dead body and the lake, the leaves would get dispersed by the wind and eventually scatter the evidence. They had gone too far off the path for anyone to wander near Angela's remains.

# Chapter 4:

Within forty-eight hours of Angela's murder, her decomposing heart started producing a horrible smell.

Each time Mrs. Duff walked into her adoptive son's bedroom, she would complain about the awful odour and ask that he open one of his windows to ventilate his room.

Jack had hidden the plastic container under his bed, amongst other things, but knew that he would have to find a better place for it soon.

When Jack opened the lid to admire the memory of his work, he realised that he had picked the wrong type of trophy. He would have to get rid of it before it was found. But, he did not like the idea of parting with it. If only he had his own private refrigerated box that he could lock up with a unique key.

After burying the heart in the backyard, Jack took a mental note to take organs that remained intact next time. He thought about his options; nails, teeth, blood drops, locks of hair. They were all things he would obviously have to hide, but could easily keep.

Since he had to get rid of his original trophy, Jack felt he needed a replacement. He could not go back into the woods to try and find Angie. But he had a few pictures of her lying around.

Jack chose one of the worst; Angie in a white string bikini that did not flatter her bony figure. He wrote her full name and date of death behind the standard sized print, added the letters R.I.P inside a drawn fancy tombstone, and placed it inside the cardboard shoebox from his mother's latest purchase. He wanted to add a few personal notes, but would have no logical explanation for them if his souvenir box was ever found and opened.

If it were examined as is, at least he could tell people that his current writing and image was his way of saying goodbye to Angie.

Talking to a coffin-like shoebox could be his symbolic way of dealing with his loss since there were no graves to visit yet. So, he even had an explanation for keeping the picture hidden inside an empty box instead of on display somewhere.

Of course, he might be asked why he believed that Angie was dead rather than missing. He thought of an answer for that too; she was gone for much too long. Surely even the police would come to the same conclusion.

If, by some devilish miracle her body was found and a proper funeral was held for her, Jack would just use the comfort story to explain his odd box. His excuse would be that he had gotten so used to talking to Angie that way that it was just easier to continue communicating like that rather than visiting her in a depressing cemetery.

Jack had never actually set foot inside a graveyard, but he heard the way people talked about them.

He didn't understand why the majority of people were so spooked since everyone in them were dead, but he would find out about the fear of zombies and ghosts soon enough. He didn't believe in them any more than he believed in the Tooth Fairy or the Easter Bunny, but his conscience would eventually put ideas in his already deranged head.

# Chapter 5:

Jack had an urge to kill again, but with Angela having been officially reported missing he knew he had to be careful.

He satisfied himself by gutting small animals, mostly neighbourhood pets, and pocketing their claws as souvenirs. In a way, it was practice for him.

As he would cut open the unfortunate creatures, he would chant: "Knife goes in, knife goes out, guts come out, blood EVERYWHERE!!!" His strange directives and verbalized observations were always followed by a demented laugh.

He added each new trophy to his shoebox and talked to Angie each time he opened his special box. He would tell her how good it felt to take away lives because it gave him power. He felt like a god when he decided to make one creature or another breathless forever. But nothing compared to ending a human life.

Killing soulless animals got old pretty fast. Jack wanted to kill another human being soon.

During a short weekend family trip to the city of Toronto, Jack found what appeared to be part of a human femur hidden in the collection of rocks beside Ontario Lake.

Mr. And Mrs. Duff believed it to be the broken bone of a large animal, but Jack knew better. He insisted on bringing the dry bone fragment to the police station.

According to the news, several other human bones were discovered under the rocks and in the polluted water. It appeared that all the bones, forming several unfinished skeletons, had been boiled to remove the muscles.

A dangerous cannibal sect was reported in the area. The idea of eating human meat fascinated Jack from that point on.

He became eager to try out a cannibalistic recipe he had recently found on the Internet. He read that human flesh tasted just like pork and wondered if it was true.

# Chapter 6:

When the news of Angela's disappearance quieted down, Jack found another unlucky victim; a snobby and conceited boy nobody would miss. Jack had no connections to him whatsoever, so he would not be questioned this time.

Having the police ask him about Angela so soon after her murder had been very stressful. At first, he was only asked basic questions such as "When did you last see her?" Jack lied of course.

He made up a story that he and Angela had walked home from school together on the Friday, and that he had not heard from her since she had left his house before dinner. He had kissed her goodbye and watched her walk down his driveway and turn right to continue on the sidewalk.

Afterwards, the police started asking more intense questions. He answered each one of them while acting as though he deeply missed Angela and would do anything to help find her. Jack even managed to form tears and allowed them to fall down his cheeks.

Mr. Duff had to ask Officer Dunham to leave because he did not like to see his son being treated like a criminal. He wanted to co-operate, but it was obvious to him that Jack was troubled by his girlfriend's disappearance and he did not need to be harassed. Mrs. Duff agreed with her husband and comforted Jack while slowly rubbing his back with a circular motion.

Officer Dunham made a quick apology and left the house after giving Jack his business card. "If you remember anything that can be of any help, please call me", he had told the teenage boy and his parents. It was his usual line, but he still felt awkward saying it.

Jack was never an official suspect, but knew that he was being watched by many. Even though he had the reputation of being a non-rebellious wiz kid, his odd interests and strange behaviour suddenly seemed questionable.

He realised that he would have to tone down some of his scientific excitement and perhaps ensure that his grades became slightly lower. How could he still study hard and focus in class while his beloved was still missing? He had started acting a little bit more depressed and worried as soon as the investigation had started, and would have to keep up the charade for a while longer.

Jack saw fifteen year old Jason O'Connor walking home from school alone and asked the smart looking teenager if he could help him with his science homework.

Jack had exceptionally good grades in everything except for his gym class, but the snob did not know that.

Jason said no to the stranger at first, but quickly changed his mind once Jack threatened his life with a pocket knife. He pretended to be desperate for better grades and in need of a smart tutor.

The two boys walked at a fast pace into the nearby woods and took out their schoolbooks from their crammed backpacks.

Jack cut Jason's throat when the boy had his back turned towards him. The body fell on the hard ground, near a muddy puddle, with a satisfying thump. "If a corpse falls but nobody is there to hear it, does it still make a sound?" Jack asked himself.

After his humorous thought, he collected some of the boy's orange-red hair as a keepsake and placed it inside the small see through Ziploc bag his mother had originally packed his sandwich in.

Afterwards, he pulled the boy's tight pants halfway off. He cut off the boy's genitals and opened them up to study. Jack got bored within seconds and dropped the organs in the mud, making a light splash.

Jack turned Jason around and cut a piece of his behind with his hunting knife.

Back home, he placed the freshly cut meat inside a baking pan, put it in the gas oven at a high temperature and let it cook.

When his mother got home, he told her he had had a strange craving for ham and took the liberty of starting dinner. Mrs. Duff thanked Jack with a pleasant smile. She turned down the temperature of the oven and added a few slices of juicy pineapple to the human ham before starting on the vegetables.

Everyone thought the ham was divine. Jack smiled at the knowledge that humans did in fact taste like pork. It wasn't the exact same taste, but similar enough to fool his family.

The evening news showed a picture of a missing thirteen year old boy the following day.

A male reporter stated that the local police believed that Jason O'Connor's disappearance was related to that of Angela Turquote's and that a child molester might be involved in the two kidnappings. However, it was too early to say for sure. A white van had been spotted circling high schools. A warning was sent out to teenage boys and girls to be on the lookout and to report anything suspicious right away.

Jack laughed internally at how wrong the police were.

Officer Dunham, or any other police officer, did not pay him a visit this time, so Jack figured that he was safe to kill again.

# Chapter 7:

Jack wanted to find another female he could open up because it had been too dark to really take a good look at Angie's sexual organs.

He needed to examine the insides of a female the same way he had briefly studied male genitals, but knew that he would have to build trust and bring a naïve girl out to the middle of nowhere again.

If he wanted to do it right, he would also have to study exactly where to cut and what to look for more extensively before he removed a reproductive system.

Of course, he would be bloody in the end. So, he needed a water source nearby.

Men were much easier to examine! But he had more interest in cutting open another girl, and even more so, in participating in another cannibalistic activity.

Jack asked a few girls out but he was turned down each time. He hoped he could discreetly follow a girl the same way he had done with Jason, but they all traveled in packs. It was hard to get any of them alone at any given time.

Since Jack still needed to kill and taste new human meat, he started stalking a fourteen year old boy by the name of Alex Rydder. This particular guy made fun of everyone on a regular basis, even though he would have been the object of ridicule himself had his parents not been filthy rich.

On the way home one afternoon, when he thought it was safe to act, Jack quickly ran to the boy and told him in a panicky voice that they were both being followed by a strange man driving a van. Trusting Jack, Alex ran with him into the woods to hide.

Once again, Jack took out his hunting knife and slit his prey's throat while he trustingly had his back turned.

Had Alex taken a few more steps forward before being murdered, he would have seen Jason's dead body. Jack almost wished he had not killed Alex so soon because he might have enjoyed seeing ultimate fear on the boy's face.

However, Alex might have screamed bloody murder and gone running farther away, not staying in one spot long enough for Jack to harm him without risking failure.

Jack took home the boy's tongue and cooked it up with chopped up green onions and fresh garlic.

When his mother came home, she was surprised to see that her son had been making food for himself again. Jack offered his mother a piece of the meat he was eating, which she tasted out of politeness and added that it was very good.

After his satisfying snack, Jack took out the see-through Ziploc bag containing the black hair he had collected from Alex and placed it in his souvenir box.

Jack excitedly told Angela about his new addition, just like he had detailed the way he had killed Jason. He could have sworn he heard her talk back to him so he told her to shut up and quickly closed the lid of the box.

After talking to the dead, Jack took out some white paper and made three comics. Each one illustrated one of his murders.

Angie's strips included the burial of her decomposing heart. Jason and Alex's comics detailed the consumption of the boys' body parts in humorous ways. When Jack was finished, he quickly threw them in his souvenir box.

Jack heard Angie's calm voice again. It seemed to have surrounded his bedroom instead of being confined inside the shoebox. Jack looked around, half scared, and decided that his mind was playing tricks on him.

The evening news reported another mysterious disappearance.

Alex Rydder, son of the famous surgeon Dr. Rydder, never made it home from school. Police believed him to be the third abduction of Mr. X.

Mrs. Duff looked very worried and told her son to be careful. She advised him to walk home with a friend if possible, or to go home with one of them and that she would pick him up on her way back from work.

If only she knew the truth!

One week later, Jason and Alex's decomposing bodies were both found, surrounded by black flies and other insects.

A hiker had gone into the woods and was lead outside his usual path by his pet dog. The black Labrador had smelled the dry blood and followed the scent in a rush. His owner met him at the unexpected crime scene.

The story made major headlines. The newspapers wrote about the boys missing parts, concluding that the killer had taken them as souvenirs. The same was verbalized on television.

While listening to the six o'clock news, Jack's mother did not say or do anything that indicated she had made a connection with her son's sudden interest in cooking and the boys' missing organs. However, Jack was afraid that she might clue in eventually. Mrs. Duff was an intelligent woman.

Jack told Angie about his concern. His dead girlfriend sarcastically asked him why he did not get rid of his mother the way he had done with her.

Angie always asked a lot of annoying questions, but this was a good one, even if the fact that she was responding to him was probably just in his head.

Jack thanked the glossy picture he was looking at and pondered on how he could accomplish his new goal.

While he thought about his options, Jack heard the echoing voices of Angie, Jason and Alex asking him what they had done to deserve such horrible deaths. Mrs. Duff caught her son talking back to invisible beings on several occasions.

# Chapter 8:

Jack decided it was time to kill his mother. Of course, he would have to kill his father as well. He felt a little bit bad about it, but his survival depended on it.

He had thought about using a pillow to suffocate his parents in their sleep, but did not want to arise suspicion amongst the police. He did not want to become a suspect in their sudden deaths, as he was sure that Officer Dunham would not take pity on him.

After putting some serious thought into his plan of action, Jack decided to stage his mother's suicide and fake his father's heart attack.

While his father slept peacefully, Jack injected pure air into his easy to find veins with an empty syringe he had discreetly stolen from the children's hospital's stock room. This caused Mr. Duff's heart to stop almost instantly.

Mrs. Duff was a heavy sleeper who could not be woken up at night, not even by a screaming fire alarm. Jack used this to his advantage.

Jack turned his mother on her back and pulled her closer to the edge of the queen size bed. He then sat behind her head, almost touching the decorative headboard, and wrapped a thick rope around her neck. Placing his feet on her shoulders, he pushed her away from him with his legs. He did this while pulling the rope tightly towards him. In less than thirty seconds, she was strangled to death.

Although it would have been much easier to just cut off her air supply with a pillow, as originally planned, hanging her afterwards would have left an implausible mark on her neck. It would have been evident that her time of death occurred before the hanging, and Jack did not want to risk anyone making this discovery. He was actually starting to be afraid of Officer Dunham.

After his satisfying murders, Jack prepared a proper noose for his mother with the same rope he had killed her with, and hung her lifeless body in the garage. It was a lot heavier than he had expected, but he managed to carry her to the desired location and hoist her up like a puppet.

He did not bother writing up a fake suicide note because he didn't really know what to say. Plus, he feared that he would not be able to mimic her handwriting correctly. Forging her signature had always been easy, but Mrs. Duff had a very neat way of writing. Jack had never gotten into any trouble before, but nobody had ever compared his fake notes to his mother's handwriting before.

Jack went back up the stairs to get his father and dragged his dead weight towards the garage.

He took the time to collect hair from his parents and placed it in individual bags before throwing the goodies inside his shoebox.

As he opened the lid, Angie congratulated him on a job well done, but asked how he was going to explain the scenario. Jason and Alex helped Angie create slight paranoia within Jack, but the killer took a few deep breaths and had everything under control.

When poor Jack came home from the library to find his mother hanging from the garage ceiling rail and his father passed out on the cold cement floor, as he told the 9-1-1 operator, he tried to resuscitate his father but it was too late. The C.P.R skills he had learned as a Boy Scout were useless in that moment.

Jack appeared to be in a state of shock when police arrived.

"I don't understand", he kept whispering with teary eyes. He didn't want to overdo it by letting everyone know how happy both his parents had always been. He was forced to speak about his family life anyways. For once, he was able to tell the whole truth.

His mother had her ups and down, but he never saw her cry. She seemed to be a fairly optimistic person who hardly ever complained about anything. His parents were very much in love...

Jack later discovered that his mother had been taking anti-depressants, which worked in his murderous favour.

It was Mrs. Duff's best friend Christine who brought it up to the police, and they found the bottle of Prozac in her medicine cabinet. Her family doctor had prescribed them, but Mrs. Duff was not seeing a psychologist. She had never shown any signs of wanting to commit suicide, but sometimes these things were overlooked.

Jack was told several times by Officer Dunham not to blame himself for his parents' deaths. He was a lot different from the last time Jack had seen him. Officer Dunham was more sympathetic and did not have an accusing tone when he spoke.

Since the Duff's house became a minor crime scene, Jack was asked if there was any family he could temporarily stay with. He told the police he had no nearby relatives, but could probably stay at his friend Jeremy Rennold's house.

He called Jeremy and explained the situation to him. His shocked friend passed the phone over to his stepmother, who told Jack that she was on her way to pick him up.

Jack packed a bag of clothes and toiletries. He did not want to leave his souvenir box behind, so he brought it with him.

Jeremy caught him talking to it several times, so Jack told him the box was filled with his parents personal items and that he needed to dwell in his own way. Jeremy thought his friend was a bit odd, but also understood him in a way so he left Jack alone with his used shoebox whenever he found him with it.

Jeremy was concerned when he overheard Jack say the name Angie. Jack explained that he was still sad about his missing girlfriend and did not believe that she would be found alive. He cried in front of his friend.

Jeremy and the rest of his family felt sorry for Jack. They were all very kind to him and helped him cope with his losses.

No proof of foul play was ever found. Mrs. Duff's suicide was accepted. Mr. Duff's autopsy's result showed that he had a heart attack, most likely caused by the sight of his wife's dangling body.

Jack took the time to open his souvenir box and childishly stick his tongue out at Angie, Jason and Alex. "I knew I could pull it off!" he told them. He got frustrated at their lack of response, but controlled his anger. He should not show his violent side.

He reminded himself on a daily basis that he had to be like Dr. Jekyll in society rather than Mr. Hyde. He needed to control his other personality and prevent it from being seen by anyone he could not kill at once.

After the Duff's funeral, Jack was informed that he had inherited all of his adoptive parents' money, their house, everything inside the home, plus additional life insurance benefits.

However, he was too young to be a homeowner and would be unable to pay the property taxes and other bills that came with owning a house. It was auctioned off, along with the furniture and valuables.

The money from the auction as well as his heritage was put into an account for Jack. He could only touch the money when he reached the age of eighteen, as instructed in Mr. and Mrs. Duff's last signed will.

# Chapter 9:

Jack was sent to a foster home. He did not have to change his last name again. However, he had to share his living space and attention with three other children, whom he did not get along with very well.

Ten year old Sally Jonson got on his nerves because she was terrified of the dark and always needed multiple lights to be on. One was not enough, because it could burn out at any moment. She always kept a working flashlight and extra C batteries with her; never rechargeable ones because their recycled energy drained too quickly. She kept her fresh batteries inside their package so that she could easily verify the expiration date.

Sally refused to step outside at night, which meant that the foster family could never go camping like his past adoptive family did every summer. Evening excursions were out for Sally, except during Daylight Savings Time. But she had to be back home before the sun set. Sally never went out until the sun had risen. She was the complete opposite of a vampire.

Her parents had been murdered in their home, while six year old Sally watched the dark shadow of the tall man stabbing them with a long kitchen knife. He spared her, but told her he would be back for her one day. Although there had been several suspects arrested, they were all let go. The killer still wandered the streets, so Sally had been living in fear for the last four years of her life.

Twelve year old Jake Ragner had been longing for a brother all his life and looked up to Jack.

At first, Jack liked his little admirer and protected him from the teasing neighbourhood kids who made fun of his short stature, but being followed around all the time soon became annoying.

Plus, he hated the fact that their names were similar. When his mother or father would shout for one of them to come see them, it was often hard to tell which one was being summoned. Jack would get a lecture if he ignored them, but felt irritated when he got up for nothing.

Jake was really Mr. and Mrs. Ragner's nephew, but he had known them as Mom and Dad since he was three.

After shooting his cheating wife, Jake's dad shot himself in the head, leaving blood and brain chunks all over the main bedroom's wallpaper.

Jake was used to other children coming and going, but often felt abandoned. He wanted stability, and somebody he could hang on to forever.

Fourteen year old Abigail Crammer was a major drama queen who needed to be in the spotlight all the time. She was obnoxious, extremely bossy and controlling. At least, she was that way with Jack and the other children. Mr. and Mrs. Ragner saw her as a perfect foster daughter and role model for Sally.

Although she had been sexually abused by her former stepfather night after night after her mother died in a tragic plane crash, Abby was a very sexual girl. She came on to Jack on several occasions, telling him that it was ok for them to have sex because they were not really related. It took a lot of effort for Jack not to kill her or rape her with a sharp object.

Jack knew that the Mr. Hyde in him had to remain dormant for a while now. He had gotten away with a lot so far, but did not feel that he would be lucky enough to avoid serious suspicion if another dead or mutilated body was found.

# Chapter 10:

Jack and his foster siblings were forced to do art as a form of therapy. To make his new hippy-like parents happy, he made an effort to draw on command.

His first picture, that of a woman hanging from a noose with a man lying by her feet, brought on many questions.

Jack had to talk to a social worker once a week about how his parents' deaths had affected him. He had to speak about his feelings and was asked to try focusing on the good memories instead of keeping a mental image of the night he found his parents dead. Jack found the therapy sessions quite boring and did the exact opposite of what he was told, by keeping his drawing among his other morbid souvenirs.

Eventually, he drew gruesome pictures of Jason and Alex. He told his social worker that the memories of the brutal murders in his former neigh-bourhood brought on terrible nightmares. He dramatically ripped up his drawings in front of the social worker, as he worked up a fit of rage.

When Jack drew the portrait of a young girl with her insides all around her, the social worker asked him what the new drawing meant. Jack told him it was a horrible vision he had in his sleep. Deep down, he was teasing the social worker and hoped that nobody would ask him to do any more thera-peutic drawings. He wanted to keep his artwork to himself.

Unfortunately, Jack was asked to make more art. He ended up drawing more gutted women and said that they were all prostitutes. "I see these images in my sleep," he confessed. This time, he was actually speaking the truth. He did not know who any of the women were, and yet all the faces he drew seemed rather familiar to him.

Because he was not discouraged to continue drawing such morbid pic-tures, Jack reproduced many more and was no longer afraid to expose his de-ranged thoughts on paper.

All the woman in his new drawings looked old fashioned in terms of their clothing style. The more he drew, the more he felt like it meant something. Of course, he did not share this with anyone. He was afraid of the explanation that might be given to him.

Jack's household thought that he was drawing such horrors because of all the trauma he had been through. Sally frequently drew pictures of dark men carrying long kitchen knives. Jake sometimes drew pictures of men with handguns. Abby's pictures were disturbing in another kind of way. She was obsessed with sex, and often drew herself in various states of seduction. Her drawings became pornographic.

Jack eventually took a new liking to his pencils and papers. He even started using dark pastels from time to time. He kept sketchpads with him and drew the human body inside and out whenever he got bored.

He openly drew fantasy murders without fear and nobody scolded him for it because he was supposedly just putting his bad dreams on paper. People did not know he was actually drawing what he willingly imagined, so they just shook their heads and said "Poor Jack". For some reason, the words "poor Annie" flashed in his mind when he overheard that.

His school art teacher called Mrs. Ragner once to let her know about Jack's disturbing drawings and paintings, but all his foster mother told him was to keep his therapy art inside the home.

Jack started reproducing nicer looking portrait in class, but always hid a tiny morbid figure somewhere. He initialled all his work on the bottom right corners of his canvases or papers like normal artists did, but his real signature became the miniscule hidden drawings nobody else could really see. They became little illusions. People saw what they wanted to see. Only Jack knew the true nature of his secret tiny images. Sometimes he was obvious, but nobody caught on.

He once painted an eight by ten acrylic picture of a devilish looking boy eating ham. The title of the work was called "Jason". People just presumed that it was the boy in the picture's name. They were only half right. The same blind hint was applied to his watercolour portrait entitled "Alex". This painting was of a boy frying up a big tongue, which appeared to be a normal piece of fat meat. He told his teacher that he was always hungry in her class. That wasn't a lie. His art class took place right before lunch and his stomach always made itself heard.

As an alternative to public art, Jack started writing out his fantasies and claimed that he was working on a thriller. He actually considered publishing a novel, but wanted to keep a low profile when it came to his dark mind. He planned on making his works of fiction real one day, and did not want anyone to see the similarities between his published words and the bodies that would be found. He doubted that he could blame his future murders on badly influenced readers.

When Jack got bored of all his unfinished short stories, he started writing poems. They were mostly about dark shadows moving about and killing women while policemen practically gave their positions away with an unwilling warning or slept close by as the murders happened. Jack wrote about blind watchmen and foolish officers.

Jack never showed his writing to anyone.

He only told a horror story once, because he was asked to write a moral story and present it in class. The only thing he could come up with was a drunk driver getting into a car accident, causing the death of his own friends. The idea was good, but he had focused on the blood and guts spilling out of the passengers of the car, more than the actual moral of the story.

The teacher made him stop his presentation when he got to the part were the inebriated driver woke up from being unconscious to find his best friend lying on the paved road with his head smashed open, leaving bits of brain matter on the gravel.

Jack did not get the chance to tell the classmates how the right arm of the body suddenly moved forward, and how it tried to get up. His friends had begged him to finish his story after class though. They thought it was awesome and encouraged him to write more zombie-like tales. It really wasn't Jack's style though.

His assignment was based on a true story he had read about, and he fluffed it up using part of a movie he recently watched. He found nothing amusing about the dead coming back to life. In fact, he kind of feared that thought because it made him wonder what his victims would do if they lived again.

Angie, Jason and Alex stopped talking to him and the Duff's had never spoken, but Jack had not opened his shoebox since he moved in with the Ragners.

Jack developed a rather punky look for himself. He pierced his left ear in five different places, got himself a tongue ring, and dyed his short, curly hair blue. He wore dark clothing and silver chains. For some reason he did not understand, girls became attracted to his bad boy side.

He started dating a gothic girl who was into pain. She let him cuff her, use other forms of bondage, tape her mouth shut… She even let him cut her with blades on occasions and had no problem with him wrapping his hands around her neck when they had sex. His only problem was that she had a dominating side that Jack never enjoyed. He needed to be in charge all the time.

The first time his girlfriend wanted to use a whip on him, he ripped it from her hand and whipped her instead. The relationship did not last.

Because it was offered to him, Jack smoked a little bit of pot from time to time. He stole cigarettes from his foster parents once, but didn't like it as much. Jack did acid a few times, which seemed to illuminate his imagination. People thought Jack was creepy when he was doing drugs or drinking alcohol because he claimed to see ghosts, but it was the only time he felt like he could really be himself without being analyzed.

Everyone was more animated when they were not sober, and Jack felt like he didn't have to hide as much when other people who were drunk or high surrounded him. He felt more out of place not following everyone's lead for once.

# Chapter 11:

Jack continued to draw pictures of mutilated women for his home therapy sessions. He also drew dead faces of women he had never met, creepy autopsy scenes, pictures of British police officers beside one butchered woman or another, a naked female torso, an old city he had never seen, a street map of the same poor city, old buildings, men in top hats. He drew what was inside his head and did not comprehend where all of it was coming from.

During a history class, Jack and his classmates were told the brief story of Jack the Ripper as a Halloween treat.

Mr. Thompson started his lesson by informing his students that Jack the Ripper was one of the most famous unsolved mysteries because the identity of the killer is still debated.

The attentive class was then told about five of the 19th century murders that occurred in the Whitechapel district of London. The five major victims were listed on the blackboard; Mary Ann Polly Nichols, Annie Chapman, Elizabeth Stride, Catherine Eddowes and Mary Jane Kelly.

Mr. Thompson took his students back in time, describing where each one of the prostitutes had been found and in what shape their bodies were discovered.

Before his teacher could finish his sentences, Jack felt like he already knew what was about to be said. He recognised the names of the streets Mr. Thompson mentioned as those he had written on his map. Even the victims' names sounded familiar to him.

Mr. Thompson mentioned that there were other murders in the East End around the same time, but that the five unfortunates were the most accepted as being Jack the Ripper victims.

He went on about the different theories and suspects related to the case, but Jack was no longer listening. He started having inexplicable flashes in his mind that almost led him to convulse. He had to be brought to the nurse's office for eventually passing out.

At first, Jack was thought to be high on something strong, but no drugs were found on his person and he recovered pretty quickly.

Fellow students made fun of Jack for his little episode, saying he could not handle such gory stories when somebody other than himself told them, and wasn't as tough as he looked.

The evil stare Jack gave them shut them up right way. If eyes could kill, several students would have died that day. The Mr. Hyde in him was starting to sneak out unexpectedly.

After school, Jack rushed to the local library to get more information on Jack the Ripper. He could have done his research at school, but wanted privacy.

He browsed the Internet for articles on the famous killer and came across some pictures from old newspapers that were very similar to the ones he had drawn. He recognised the faces of all fourteen woman he had drawn in his therapy session. "Jack the Ripper had a lot more than five victims", he whispered to himself.

He noted down the names and the faces of the Whitechapel murder victims that were more familiar to him on one side of his sheet of paper, and noted the unfamiliar ones on the other side. He also noted the dates each body or body parts had been found.

Jack was suddenly very excited. He felt like he had found himself even if he knew it was impossible.

When Jack got home, he told his foster parents that he wanted to get in touch with his real family. Not his adoptive one, he pointed out, but his birth parents. Mr. And Mrs. Ragner agreed to help Jack track down his real parents to the best of their ability, but confessed that they really did not know where to start.

Jack started a personal search on his own.

He found his adoption papers in the scrapbook Mrs. Duff had completed for him, and phoned the orphanage to ask for copies of his records. The nice woman on the other end told him it was not uncommon for adoptive children to want to be reunited with their birth families and that she would give him as much information as she could, but that he should not be too disappointed if his birth parents did not welcome him back into their lives with open arms. Jack only wanted to find out his background. The woman told her she would find his file and send him whatever she could.

A week later, Jack received a large envelope in the mail. He found out that the Colney Hatch Asylum in London, England had released him on his tenth birthday, which he vaguely remembered now.

He always saw that home as another orphanage. Since he had never been allowed outside the walls of the asylum, he never knew that he was in London. He always thought he was Canadian. Although, he did recall everyone around him having an accent now. He must have had one at some point too, but evidently lost it.

Jack remembered his German dreams and wondered again what they were all about. Had he lived in Germany before the mental institution? He had to find out more about himself.

He wondered what he was doing in a mental institution in the first place. He could see himself being sent to one now that he was clearly not on the same page as the rest of society, but could not remember much from his early childhood. No details were mentioned in the pages that had been sent to him.

Jack made an expensive long distance call to the asylum and requested information about himself. Unfortunately, all the records were confidential and could not leave the institution. Jack was upset at not being able to obtain copies of his own files. He asked if he could at least get the name of his former psychiatrist so that he may contact him. The receptionist told him she could take his name and number and have the doctor call him when he got in. Jack hung up. There had to be a better way to dig into his past!

Jack had a dream in which he was lying on a leather couch and talking with his eyes closed. He was a young boy in the dream, but told a man wearing glasses that he was Jack the Ripper. On the man's desk, a wooden nameplate read Dr. George Philips.

His dream was interrupted by his screaming sister. Jack was angry at not being able to finish his dream, but he was grateful for the images to still be fresh enough for him to remember the name he had seen. He wrote it down on a piece of paper before he could forget.

The next day, Jack phoned the Colney Hatch Asylum and asked to speak to Dr. Philips. "Which one?" the rude receptionist wanted to know. "Dr. George Philips", Jack politely replied. She transferred Jack to Dr. Philip's extension in a rush. When the psychiatrist answered the phone, Jack recognised his deep voice and everything came back to him.

Jack remembered waking up in his mother's tearful grasp next to one of his sisters' dead body, his parents crying and shouting as they managed to take away the knife he was holding, the police that came to the house because he had viciously murdered his sweet siblings, the day he was brought to the asylum, his hour long therapy sessions, the hypnosis, and most importantly: the fact that he was Jack the Ripper.

He started a personal journal, writing down everything interesting he had gathered from his past life, and linked it to his new one. He jotted down his dreams when he woke up, as he was certain now that they were memories of his past life.

Jack was now aware that he had been born in Germany back in the eighteen hundreds. He remembered traveling to England with his past life father for nasty operations on more than one occasion, and not being able to comprehend what was going on or why.

In a flash, Jack recalled moving to England on his own as a grown man, after learning the spoken language.

In his sleep, he saw his old self randomly attacking Emma Smith because he had always wanted to stab a prostitute. He saw his doctor friend join in the fun shortly after.

Jack watched in the shadow of his conscience as he killed Martha Tabram.

He listened to Dr. Gull tell him about the Queen's fury at her son and the trouble the Royal Family was in. Behind the Queen's back, they both agreed to secretly take care of the problem.

Annie Cook, the initial cause of the Queen's anger, was taken away for Dr. Gull to treat for false insanity. Since Mary Kelly had seen the well dressed and clean shaven men take her friend away in a horse drawn carriage, Jack had the perfect excuse to kill her and her three loud mouth friends. He had made a stupid mistake with Catherine Eddowes, but did not regret it. It served her right for impersonating somebody else! Jack did not like being lied to.

Their Freemason companions covered up the mess that the doctor and Jack had done to protect the Royal Family's image. Jack had found the whole story amusing because it had been him who had introduced the Duke to Annie.

He remembered telling his wife at the time that it was all his fault that the murders took place. She originally saw his guilt in a different way than what it really was.

Jack knew his former name now; Walter Richard Sickert. He was born on May 31, 1860 and died on January 22, 1942.

He knew that little Alice Margaret, the rejected granddaughter of the Queen, was living with the nuns. He claimed to be watching over her. As she grew older, he started stalking her on a daily basis. Much later, Alice ended up giving birth to a son, Joseph, and accused him of being the father. He knew it was impossible because he was impotent, but having Annie's daughter bear his last name was amusing to him. Besides, he did not want to announce his embarrassing problem to anyone. His wife was a feminist who never wanted sex. They had a brother/sister type of relationship. Never having seen each other naked, she never found out that her husband could not have been unfaithful to her as he eventually told her he was. She believed him because he often brought prostitutes into his studios as models to paint nude portraits of them, and had a habit of disappearing for days at a time.

After Ellen divorced him years later for unrelated reasons, he married his art student Christine. She was sick when he became engaged to her, but she only died fifteen years later. He didn't really care.

He cared so little, that he did not even bother getting her headstone engraved properly. He left it on the grounds of the cemetery with the carving of her name and where it had been made, but no dates were ever carved into the green marble. He never visited her grave after she was buried.

He remembered her cheap, wooden casket breaking open during the burial, revealing her pale face and rigid body. That was a vision he was sure people would never forget, no matter how hard they tried. He himself had wanted to erase it from his thoughts because the haunting image reminded him that he had poisoned her for not dying fast enough.

The only thing he did to keep Christine's memory alive was draw a portrait of her dead body before her cremation.

He remarried another artist, Therese, four years after Christine's death. She had moved in with him shortly after the funeral.

He tried his best to keep up a good appearance despite his hatred for each woman, but his charm became less and less believable over the years.

Although Ellen had continued to take care of him after their divorce, he always suspected that she knew more about his dark side than she seemed to. She remained in his life until she died of cancer, but he always felt like she feared him. Maybe she was afraid of what he might do to her if she went public with her thoughts on whom her former husband might be. He became such a respectable man that nobody would have believed her, even if she later mysteriously disappeared like so many other women in his life.

Jack dreamt of all the women he killed, cut up, and dismembered. He recalled eating some of their flesh or organs, and spreading the rest around London and other cities. He sometimes fed the starving children with the meat.

Jack remembered taking soldier outfits from the deceased during the war. He would also draw the dead or wounded men. Nobody questioned his actions because of his profession.

One night, he dreamt of his last murder, that of Emily Dimmock, who lived in his Camden neighbourhood.

He saw her walk by regularly, and although her significant other knew nothing about the venereal disease she was spreading by selling her body, Jack was fully aware. He saw her pick up clients at The Rising Sun several times, and overheard her conversations.

On the night of September 12, 1907, he saw Emily walking by his house with curlers in her hair. He rushed outside and asked the woman if he could go home with her. Since he did not mind her attire, she let him follow her inside her house and into the bedroom. He did not want to have sex with her, but pretended to want to take her from behind. He cut her throat when she was in position and left her completely naked in her bed.

Shortly after, he placed her bed sheets over her body before cleaning himself up. He then stole the house keys that were left in the drawer and exited the home, locking each door behind him.

The following day, he asked officers what was going on. When they told him, he asked if he could draw the scene of the crime. As a well-known artist, they had no problem with it. He did several sketches, and later made a painting of the murder.

Jack's past personality had begun to be part of his present one long ago.

Aside from his criminal mind and hatred for any living human or animal he deemed useless, he had already began to sign his name is various ways without doing on purpose. In his old life, he would sign his name W.R.S, W.S. R.S, Walter R.S, W. Sickert, W.R Sickert... In his present life, he had been Jack Huntington and Jack Duff.

He was sometimes called J.D. by his close friends after his parents started calling him that to avoid him being mistaken for Jake. So, sometimes he would write his name in full, and other times he was J.D. On official documents, he signed his name J. Duff. For school, he sometimes just wrote Jack D. on papers when he was lazy. His teachers did not like him writing J.D.

Some things never changed.

Jack became secretly obsessed with who he had once been, that he filled hundreds of pages of notes on his darkest years. He wrote down so many details that he could have easily transformed his notes into a best selling novel. But too many books had been written about Jack the Ripper that it would be pointless for him to even bother. His Whitechapel murders made history, but he killed elsewhere. He could write about all of those other murders and see if anybody ever put two and two together.

While doing intensive research on his old self, Jack discovered that there were several versions of his story, but so far he had only found one author that seemed to have figured him out. It infuriated him that it was a woman.

Lucky for him, his former body had been cremated in 1942, leaving absolutely no DNA to compare from the saliva taken from some the envelopes he had licked closed back in 1888. Other DNA would be found anyways, because he sometimes asked his wife or friends to send unsealed envelopes for him. So, this smart author could not prove with one hundred percent certainty that it was him. But she was still too close to the truth and Jack wondered if he should pay her a visit.

What if she figured him out in THIS life!?! Could he be put on trial for murders he committed in a past life? That was stupid. They would have to prove that Walter Sickert was Jack the Ripper, then prove that Jack Duff was Walter Sickert in a past life. The criminal system was weird, but it wasn't that deranged! He would be found not guilty before a trial could begin, and the accuser would most likely get sent to a mental institution. Jack laughed at that thought. He breathed a little bit easier.

Since Jack wanted to become another unsolved mystery, he took notes of his past behaviours that could affect the present. When he watched suspense and crime shows, he took down notes of what investigators looked for and wrote down mistakes that killers had made so that he would not accidentally commit the same damaging errors. After watching horror movies, he wrote down ideas as they still inspired him. Nobody was stopping him from viewing bloody shows now! They had become a big part of his personality.

# Chapter 12:

Jack had always considered himself as a good actor because he convinced people on a daily basis that he was something he wasn't. He played people all the time with his fake emotions and loved it.

Nobody found out about his secret talent until he was forced to recreate a scene from Macbeth for his English class. Jack loved reading Shakespeare, but never admitted this to anyone. He pretended that it was boring and incomprehensible, yet understood every word as though he had studied it intensely before. He felt like he had already read the old Scottish play, and knew that it was probable.

Needing some fellow actors to practice his lines at home, he forced his female siblings to act out his scene. Why he chose the witches scene was beyond his male schoolmates, but Jack had been pretty insistent on it so they eventually just went with it. He had volunteered to direct everything and had proven to be highly creative.

When his sisters refused to do the scene one last time, Jack tied them up just like he had done to his past life siblings when they refused to co-operate with him. It was the only act of abuse he had inflicted upon his foster siblings so far. He had enjoyed it, but knew that he could not continue this bad behaviour. He blamed his sudden change of behaviour on his new enthusiasm for theatre. He could be whomever he wanted! Especially Walter Sickert.

Jack thought that becoming an actor might be a good career path for him, but changed his mind once he took the possible fame into consideration. He loved the attention, but did not want the spotlight lit directly on his face when he acted upon his personal fantasies.

He wanted unanimous credit for his future work without risking his face being associated with it while he was still alive. The paparazzi were crazy and would never give him the chance to step outside his home unnoticed. Times sure had changed!

Most actors never made it big, so Jack decided to act as a temporary hobby.

Jack took advantage of his potential and auditioned for the school production of Hamlet. He was given the role of the ghost.

He had fun coming on and off the stage using the trap doors, and imagined himself coming in and out of sight from future victims.

He loved the applause he received and the shouts of "Encore!" Jack pretended to be stage shy. He avoided cameras and had to be convinced to do short interviews for the local newspapers, but he loved hearing and reading about himself. He clipped articles about the productions he was in and kept tapes of the filmed shows he performed in. He had a few fans who complimented him on his acting skills.

After that, Jack often walked around his house reciting Shakespeare lines, mostly from the tragedies.

Most of his friends teased him and told him he should stop taking so many drugs. Jack thought about taking their advice, but not for the same reason they had. They wanted him to stop talking in old English; the use of the words thy and thou, along with the old style grammar were annoying.

Jack just wanted the visions of Angela, Alex, Jason and his adoptive parents to stop haunting him. They had reappeared in his life during his first drug intake, and returned to him every time he got high.

Like Hamlet's father, they would appear to him. Jack preferred being the ghost than seeing the dead.

The following year, Jack had gained popularity and cleaned himself up. Jack ran for school president and won. He wrote for the school paper as well.

He also joined a theatre troupe and persisted that they put up a production of "Jekyll and Hyde". Jack secretly compared himself to the main character and wanted to portray him on stage as a tease to everyone who thought he was an everyday normal guy with a single personality.

Instead, he requested to direct the play and had such good ideas that everyone accepted. Nobody realised that he was reproducing the 1888 version of the show.

The play was a big success and Jack was happy to see his name in numerous papers again.

# Chapter 13:

At exactly two twenty-six in the morning, according to her bedroom alarm clock, Sally left the comfort of her bed to go to the bathroom.

As she was washing her hands, she saw the reflection of a tall figure inside the mirror. When she turned around, dropping her bar of soap into the sink, it was gone. Sally had a habit of becoming jumpy when her own movements were briefly seen in the glass.

The girl's heart continued beating rapidly despite the confirmation that her vision was all in her mind; She desperately hoped it wasn't real anyways.

Sally still had to walk back to her room but was afraid to leave the comfort of her little shelter. That is, until the four light bulbs over the sink mirror stopped producing light. The small bathroom window had its blinds shut, so Sally found herself in complete darkness.

In a state of panic, the young girl opened the bathroom door and dashed towards her room. The dark hallway never seemed to end. The comforting nightlights had all been unplugged and carelessly tossed on the floor.

Inside her room, Sally came face to face with her worst nightmare. All the lights were off, and a tall man stepped out of the corner holding a long kitchen knife.

Sally woke herself up yelling "HEEEEELP!!!" in a high-pitched voice. Of course, the rest of the household was startled awake as well.

Jack was used to hearing his foster sister shout for help in the middle of the night, but still got annoyed by the fact that his sleep always seemed to get interrupted when he was having the best dreams.

He dreamed of a tall man with a knife too, but did not see his visions as nightmares at all. In fact, he loved the dreams about his past life as Jack the Ripper because he killed so many innocent women and never got caught.

Jack hoped that he could eventually start killing again and become famous, without being discovered. He couldn't wait to be old enough to live on his own and start a fun new game.

# Chapter 14:

Jack snapped. He could not longer handle Sally's complaints about the dark and the man that was after her.

He had fought the urge to kill her for several days now because of her recurring night screams. Each time he thought about stabbing the girl, he managed to control himself. He told himself that he needed to be careful and plan ahead. He had gotten away with murder before but did not want to push his luck.

In the middle of the night, he cut the power off and went up to Sally's room with the biggest knife he could find.

He woke his foster sister up by slapping her hard across the face and quickly hid beside her bed. When Sally realised that she was in the dark, she prepared herself to scream. Jack jumped out of his hiding place and covered the girl's head with a pillow. He whispered that if she made a sound he would gut her just like he had done to her parents.

Jack slowly let the pillow go as he went back into hiding.

The girl whimpered silently as tears began to pour from her frightened blue eyes. On the wall, she could see Jack's shadow slowly rising up. Sally wet herself, but did not move to get changed. Jack made sure the girl saw the shadow of his long kitchen knife before rapidly descending it into the back of her neck. He took a lock of her hair and left her on the carpeted floor with several bleeding stab wounds.

Jack crept into Abby's room and raped her. He kept his hand on her dry mouth so that she wouldn't scream and finally just cut her throat.

It was almost like reliving Angela's murder, but with the slight thrill of almost getting caught. There was nowhere to run if somebody walked into the room.

He slowly calmed down and cleaned his bloody knife with the flowered bed sheets before exiting the bedroom.

Mr. and Mrs. Ragner were next. Jack went completely crazy on them. He repeatedly stabbed them uncontrollably, creating blood smears all over the walls, floor, king sized bed, headboard, and ceiling.

After taking his usual souvenirs, Jack hid the murder weapon between the blood soaked mattresses and took his foster father's gloves off.

Since he did his work naked this time, there would be no bloody clothes to find. He simply took a quick shower and went to find Jake.

Jack spared Jake's life because he needed him as an alibi. He woke him up and told him that an intruder was inside the house. Before he could say anything more, Jake exclaimed with wide eyes: "He's after Sally!!!" Jack was happy with the boy's comment. He had hoped that Jake would come to this conclusion.

The boys ran down the stairs as fast as they could, found the front door ajar, ran outside and went to find refuge inside their next-door neighbour's house.

At the police station, Jake and Jack were taken into two separate rooms for questioning. Both boys mentioned Sally's tragic past, in their own words, and their belief that the man who had murdered Sally's parents exactly four years ago had entered their home to finish up his job, as promised.

Police records would later confirm Sally's story to be true. The night of the Ragner family's murder would have been the four year anniversary of Sally's parents murder.

Jack said that he had gotten home late, which the police could validate with the friends who had dropped him off at one in the morning. He may have forgotten to lock the door, which had become one of his bad habits. When he went upstairs, everyone was sound asleep. He took a shower, which took longer than usual because it took forever for the water to get warm. When he got out, he saw a tall man dressed in black clothing enter his parents' room. Their room was the last one on the right side of the hallway. Jack claimed to have entered Sally's room to find her mutilated. He paused before telling Officer Brown that he found Abby the same way. He ran to Jake's room, which was on the left side of the hallway, same as the bathroom. Jake looked dead because of his sleeping state, but there was no blood anywhere like the others. When Jack realised that Jake was alive, he woke him up and told him what he had seen.

Jake told the police that Jack woke him up with the frightening news that a stranger was inside the house and had already paid an unpleasant visit to their foster sisters. As they were running down the stairs, Jake saw a dark shadow in the mirror. He could tell the front door wasn't closed properly before reaching it. He ran to their neighbour Wilson's house and rang the doorbell non-stop until the door was finally opened.

When the police showed up at Mr. Wilson's address, he had admitted that it had taken Jack's hysterical shouts for help to motivate Wilson to open up his front door. He let the frightened kids in and called the police after hearing

Jack tell him in a panicked voice that his foster family had just been murdered. Jake barely said a word until he was forced to talk.

Since Jack had intelligently used a condom with Abby, his semen would not be linked to her rape. He had hidden the used condom, along with his new trophies, inside his special box so that the police would not find any evidence when searching the house. He doubted that they would take a peek inside every single closed bag, box and other storage devices in the house.

Jack had thought about planting fake evidence inside the home, but changed his mind. For one, he did not know how he would manage to obtain it. He had considered paying a prostitute to give him her last client's used condom, but was half certain that his strange request would be denied. If he managed to convince a prostitute to fulfill his dirty fantasy, the man in question would most likely dispose of the condom himself. If she managed to retrieve it from the garbage and hand it to Jack, she would definitely remember his strange request. The evidence found would be in the papers, and if the man had a valid alibi Jack's plan could backfire. He thought about obtaining hair or saliva from a random man, but the whole alibi issue worked against him once again. So, in the end he decided to rely entirely on Jake to avoid becoming a suspect.

The only thing that could potentially ruin him was if he left footmarks on his parents' thin bedroom carpet. He could explain a size eleven footprint in Sally or Abby's rooms if they were found on the side of the bed closest to the entrances, but he might be in trouble if a print matching his own feet was left elsewhere.

Jack began to get awfully anxious. He hoped that he would be able to go back to the house and examine the scenes carefully before the police sent their forensics team.

Jack got part of his wish. The boys were escorted to their home to quickly pack up a bag of clothes and essential items.

Both boys were being watched as they prepared their suitcases. Thinking fast, Jack requested to use the bathroom.

Instead of opening the first door on the left, he ran further ahead into his parents' room. He was probably planting evidence now, but he also had a witness, other than Jake, who would be able to justify them.

Jack was found near his parents' bed, unable to hold in his last intake of food. He could handle all the blood, but wanted to give out the impression that it make his stomach turn. It had been dark when he found his sisters. Now, there was sunlight shining through the large rectangular windows.

# Chapter 15:

Jack and Jake were placed in new foster homes, in different cities. Neither one knew the whereabouts of the other. They were each placed under the witness protection programme and given new identities.

Jack was stubborn about wanting to keep his first name. In the end, they gave him Jack as his middle name, as long as he went by the name Damien Rippler until the age of eighteen. He could change his name again once he reached legal age.

Jack started his new life in Ottawa, Ontario, introducing himself as Damien J Rippler. He hated the fact that the police kept a close eye on him and his family "for his own safety", and half wished that he had taken the time to frame somebody for his last set of murders.

As far as he knew, not a single suspect has been brought in yet! Until somebody was found guilty, Jack would have to endure his new undercover bodyguards.

He remembered how easy it had been to put the blame on other people in the past. People barely looked at all the facts before pointing fingers. They just took pieces of information and based accusations on what suited them. Police mainly needed to lock somebody up to appease everyone. Many unfair arrests were made and innocent prisoners paid for crimes they would never even think about committing. Now, fair trials were held and it was much harder to turn heads in the wrong direction.

Damien was starting to get discouraged. He felt like a lost Dr. Jekyll without his thrilling experience. He needed his drug and was starting to get the shakes.

# Chapter 16:

To avoid going insane, (more than he already was), Damien found a part time job at a funeral home.

The first thing he noticed when he walked into the place was that the carpets were dark red. He wondered if it had anything to do with keeping bloodstains from being visible.

Damien was hired as a basic helper, so he took care of the cleaning, watering the fresh flowers, running small errands, helped setting up, passing out programs before certain funerals, standing by with a box of Kleenex during the ceremonies…

Sometimes, he would take a quick peek at the dead bodies.

He eventually faked an interest in becoming a funeral director so that he could spend as much time in the embalming room as possible. The workers proudly showed him the basics as he took notes.

Damien stole edible organs from time to time after autopsies where performed. He tasted kidneys, tongue (again!), liver, and intestines. He avoided eating any part of the human brain because he had read somewhere that it could make a person go crazy. Even if it might just be an urban legend, Damien avoided it like the plague.

Once, a body came in so mutilated that Damien took a few chunks of meat from the legs and arms without anybody noticing. He cooked it in a stew with several healthy vegetables and got really sick that night.

Damien had no problem staying away from non-fresh meat after that. In fact, he became a vegetarian. Everyone was subjected to his bullshit story that he was against animal cruelty and refused to eat anything that once had a face.

As a stupid joke, one of his new friends asked him if he wanted fries and cooked up some McCain Smileys. Sam gave Damien the plate of hot fries shaped like happy faces and apologized sarcastically for serving him something that had a face.

Damien did not appreciate being made fun of, and got the boy back by feeding him a human meat sandwich a few days later. He really wanted to tell Sam what he was eating in an apologetic tone, but instead he just said that he was sorry for feeding him something out of the ordinary. Sam presumed that it was some sort of tofu substance and continued to devour his surprisingly savoury snack.

# Chapter 17:

During a funeral, Damien spotted a plain looking girl around his age.

After the ceremony, he walked up to her to bring her some comfort. It had become part of his job to say soothing words whenever it felt right. The mourning girl told Damien her name was Angie Morison.

A flash of Angela's murder went through Damien's head, but he remained neutral as Angie explained to him how her Aunty Janis was like a second mother to her and that she would miss her very much. Since she started crying hysterically, Jack took her in his strong arms and told her that everything would be all right.

Angie's younger sister Nadia passed by minutes later to tell her they were leaving for the family get-together. Damien didn't think it would be appropriate to ask Angie out on a date at this moment, but he wanted to see her again. He faked a headache and requested to leave work early. The funeral director let him go. Damien followed all the vehicles, driving the grey Honda he often borrowed from his new parents, and took note of the address they parked in front of.

If he killed the sister, he thought, he would see Angie again at another funeral. It would be tough to lose his annoying bodyguards, but he was sure that he could come up with an excuse to ask them for some breathing room. After all, he was seventeen years old now. Any boy his age would hate to be followed around by people being paid to protect him. It was an ego buster.

Damien had no luck convincing his two protectors to keep their distance. He got into a fight with one of them and asked if he was allowed to go to the bathroom in peace, which only made the muscular man laugh.

Damien's assigned bodyguards only followed him outdoors or inside crowded public places, but they were being discreet and felt that they were already giving him too much space. It wasn't safe to keep their guard down.

Using the oldest trick in the book, Damien snuck out of his bedroom window one Saturday night. He slept in the basement, so it wasn't that hard. All he had to do was climb onto his five drawer dresser using a chair and open the small wide window. He made sure to keep the screen-less window slightly open with a tree branch so that he could go back in later.

The tricky part was remaining unnoticed by his stupid guards. Damien felt like he was escaping prison.

Since his bedroom window faced the back yard, he decided to jump the metal fence and head towards his backyard neighbour's street.

When he arrived in front of his target home, Damien watched from across the street as Nadia put her reading material down on her white nightstand and closed her pink princess lamp.

Damien waited patiently in some bushes for Nadia's parents to turn off all the other lights in the house and go to bed themselves.

When he felt it was safe, Damien started throwing small pebbles at the girl's bedroom window. Seeing that it did nothing in terms of alerting anyone, he threw a big rock at it, shattering the glass and ripping part of the black bug screen.

Damien went back into hiding, just in case the noise woke anybody up. He stayed put for an hour despite the pouring rain, wondering what to do next. He hadn't figured out how he was going to get to the second floor window.

When he saw the giant vines of leaves along the side of the house, an idea sprang into his devious mind.

He climbed up the sturdy wood grate holding all the vines against the brick wall and made his way on the flat roof of the garage. Peeking into Nadia's bedroom, he established that she was sound asleep and that he was safe to enter.

Damien had no problem leaving muddy prints inside because he had bought a pair of boots one size too big for him, and did not intend on keeping them after this night. The heavy rain automatically washed away the footprints he made outside as he stepped out of them. The obstacle was trying not to get caught on the cut glass. He had to make sure that his own blood or clothing fibres were not left behind.

Too late to turn back now! He was getting really desperate to see Angie again.

With his gloved hands, Damien took off what he could of the broken glass, made a bigger hole out of the screen and went inside Nadia's small room. Sneaky as a snake, he moved towards the girl's single bed and completed his task.

The next morning, Nadia's body was found with her throat slit and with several stab wounds to her abdomen.

As Damien predicted, the Morison family came back to the funeral home he worked at. Damien made himself available for teary eyed Angie, and hypocritically told her how terribly sorry he was for her loss.

During the second Morison funeral, Damien looked around the room at all the family members. He noticed that Grandpa was in a wheelchair and looked deader than Nadia. If it weren't for his constant twitch of the head and the occasional movements of his shaking hands, it would appear that he should be inside the polished wooden coffin instead of the ten year old girl.

Damien took a mental note of Grandpa's state. It might come in handy if Angie did nothing to show that she wanted to see Damien again.

Two whole months went by before Damien visited Grandpa Morison's nursing home. He killed the old man the same way he had killed his foster dad, by injecting air into his veins and allowing the heart to stop. This time, he has stolen a syringe from the garbage of a local medical clinic. It was used, but he didn't care.

Damien left without announcing the death. After all, he never told the receptionist that he was going to visit Mr. Morison. He was lucky that his new foster grandparents lived in the same home, because his bodyguards had kept an even closer watch on him since Nadia's murder.

Damien was not a suspect, but his protectors thought that the killer might be the same one as the Ragner family's murderer. They were not wrong.

The thought that Damien was being protected by people who were technically trying to put him behind bars made him laugh a little bit. It's a good thing that nobody ever went through his stuff because his souvenir box now had a piece of Grandpa Morison's grey hair as well as a lock of Nadia's golden blond curls in it.

Poor Angie found Damien on her own when she entered the funeral home for her third sad event of the year. "I'm glad to see you", she confessed. "So am I", Damien replied. "I just wish that we could stop meeting under such horrible circumstances". Angie took the bait and asked him if he would like to meet her outside the funeral home some time. Damien told her yes. He maintained low enthusiasm though.

The night Angie and Damien were supposed to go see a romantic movie together, Angie called to cancel their date. Damien told her he understood, but was furious inside. She never rescheduled.

Damien stalked the girl for weeks and killed her when he managed to spot her alone on her way home one evening. He had become an expert at sneaking out of his room and did so whenever he had the chance.

When he noticed Angie walking by herself, Damien became quite violent on the sidewalk. He almost forgot that it wasn't safe to kill in the open like that. Stabbing somebody right under a lit streetlight was no stroke of genius. He fled the scene in a panic, not taking the time to collect a strand of hair.

Damien left his knife behind a few streets later. Maybe it would help. Damien made sure to run east of the house first, and then head back west towards his home.

The Morison family made their last visit to the funeral home, while Damien was still employed there.

He was accused of being a necrophiliac because he got caught kissing Angie's cold lips when he thought he was alone with the corpse. Damien made excuses that he was simply saying goodbye to his friend, but the funeral director did not like the boy's behaviour. He noticed the boy had some of the dead girl's blond hair in his hands and sent him away.

# Chapter 18:

Damien found another part time job in a small butcher shop.

He told everyone that he didn't like his new job because of all the dead animals hanging in the big walk-in freezer and the bloody apron the butcher always wore, but he secretly loved it.

His adoptive father, Mr. Duff, used to take him hunting every year and they would always prepare the meat themselves. When the butcher had to cut one part or another, Damien would watch and take mental notes. It wasn't much different than what his dad used to do with the deer and moose they would kill, but the anatomy of the cows and pigs were still a bit different.

Damien pretended to be grossed out by the butcher's work, but he really enjoyed it. Seeing all the blood made him salivate and go hungry like a lion.

He wondered what it would be like to hang a human body on the large meat hooks and let them bleed out like animals. Maybe he would have the chance to try it out one day. Damien smiled at the thought.

Oliver, the fat butcher, caught Damien in a daydream as the boy sat alone at the cash register. He made fun of him and asked him who the lucky girl was. Damien had no answer so Oliver just left laughing.

Normally, Damien would have had the impulse to seek revenge. But he would rather people think that his head was in the clouds because of a pretty girl than because of a dead one.

After a month of working at the butcher shop, with the benefit of being able to purchase fresh meat at a highly discounted price, Damien turned savage again.

He brought home a thick red beefsteak and ate it all, leaving his mixed vegetables and baked potato on his plate. He even chewed on the bone and sucked the marrow out.

Damien soon became a full time meat eater again. His family and friends made fun of him for abandoning his morals, but he did not care in the least.

He had much bigger flaws than being an omnivore like most of the human population.

# Chapter 19:

Damien sat in his grade twelve biology class, wishing that his replacement teacher would just shut up before his head exploded.

The sound of her voice was worst than hearing fingernails sliding down on a chalkboard. The prolongation of her letter S before and after her words became more and more irritating. If she did not seal her lips soon, Damien was going to pounce on her and make her voiceless.

He already knew everything she was showing the class and just wanted her to give them their assignment already!

His head started throbbing from the pain Mrs. Montgomery was causing him. When she went from one side of the chalkboard to the other, her walk annoyed Damien beyond belief.

Damien realised that even her slow movements irritated him. Did she have to slowly turn her head to look at the entire class before every single note she wrote on the board? It appeared like she was inspecting every student through her tiny glasses to made sure everyone was fully paying attention.

Unable to stand Mrs. Montgomery any longer, Damien asked to be excused to go to the bathroom.

Inside one of the locked stalls, he took out his Swiss army knife and carved his frustrations away on the side wall.

He made a cartoon portrait of Mrs. Montgomery holding her throat with bulging eyes. If he would of had a red marker with him, he would have coloured in some blood coming from the cartoon's throat. Without that added touch, his picture looked like the woman was choking herself with her bare hands.

When Damien returned to his classroom, everyone including Mrs. Montgomery were completely silent. Damien couldn't even hear anybody chewing gum.

The replacement teacher sat at her temporary desk, observing the students while they worked. She opened her mouth to tell Damien what the homework was and it hit a nerve inside him. "Sssssseventy Ssssixsss is the page you must read to answer the questionssss on thissss paper". She sounded almost snake like. The word "SSSasssssssy" echoed in Damien's head for an inexplicable reason. Then he remembered writing how sassy he was back in 1888.

Later that evening, Damien wanted to make his drawing come to life because he could not get the sound of Mrs. Montgomery's annoying voice out of his head.

Instead, he contented himself by looking at his past trophies while listening to classical music at an extremely high volume. Damien found this kind of music very soothing. It helped him keep the monster inside him from coming out.

Becoming Assistant Butcher also helped his compulsions, but he couldn't go crazy on the animal carcasses. He had to be very precise. This skill would come in handy one day.

# Chapter 20:

When Damien turned eighteen years old, he thought about legally changing his name back to Jack.

His initial thought was to reverse his current name, making it Jack Damien Rippler instead of Damien Jack Rippler. The second set of names sounded awful to his ear, hence why he used a middle initial from the beginning.

At a glance, he laughed out loud at what his mind saw. "Reverse my first two names, use the D as my middle initial instead of writing it in full and drop one L from my last name," he thought. "What do you get? Jack D Ripper!" Vocalized, it sounded like Jack the Ripper with a Jamaican accent.

Damien liked it, but it was too obvious. So, he simply left his name as it was and introduced himself as Jack to most people instead of Damien. He knew many people that went by their middle name.

He continued to sign his name D.J. Rippler because he had no choice (legally), but as the days went by he became Jack to the world again. The name Damien faded away.

# Part 2

## (Playtime)

# Chapter 1:

Jack took his heritage money to buy a nice black sports car and a small three bedroom house in downtown Montreal, where he would start his studies to become a doctor.

He refused to rely on basic anatomy books or verbal coaching to do his grand work like he had in his past life. He wanted proper training this time.

Jack got excellent grades. In fact, he was one of the best students at McGill University. However, Jack quit his medical studies after the seventh year because he realised how much he would hate working in a hospital.

He was originally aiming to become a surgeon so that he could cut people up in public. But, he did not feel like saving lives. He wanted to take them away. He realised that he would most likely be too tempted to kill his patients on the operating table and that would lead to too many questions and possible lawsuits.

Before his decision to back out of medicine, Jack had already begun practicing his medical methods on homeless people he would find asleep.

Jack would drag their stinking bodies into his car and drive home with the passed out man or woman. He always covered them up in case people looked in the backseat.

Sometimes, Jack would have to inject his kidnapped victims with drugs. Jack would then hang them on meat hooks, bleed them to death, and cut them open as he pleased. He would mostly mimic the operations he was being trained to do.

He would then take as much meat as he could remove and grind it for his homemade meat pies, pasta sauces, sausages and stir-fries. Essentially, Jack stopped buying ground beef and replaced it with ground human.

His freezer was filled with his own hunting successes. He would put whatever he didn't want into garbage bags and toss it into a cardboard box or two.

Jack would leave the closed boxes beside an industrial bin, but he never read or heard about body parts being discovered. He guessed that city workers threw the perfectly normal looking boxes into their trucks with the rest of the garbage.

Sometimes, Jack would have his University friends over for diner and serve them meals cooked with his special ingredient or human liver pates as an evening snack. People often told him that he should become a chef. They asked for his recipes, but he wanted to keep them a secret for obvious reasons. "A good chef never discusses his special ingredients", he would say. That was enough for people to stop pestering him for his secret recipes.

Since the house Jack purchased used to be a small family owned funeral home, morbid jokes were often made. "If this home was still in business, I would question the meat you are serving us", one of his classmates said one day. Not many people appreciated this dark humour, but Jack found it hilarious. "That's disgusting", he told his guest, but laughed internally.

The fact that Jack's house had previously served as a funeral home became very useful to Jack. He did his killings in the basement where the body preparations used to take place. Because of the drainage system in place, the blood would go directly into the main sewer system. If ever the place were scanned for blood, it would not be abnormal to find traces. He was absolutely thrilled when he found this discounted home for sale.

After obtaining as much medical knowledge as he wanted, Jack decided to finish a degree where he could teach science instead of obtaining a medical diploma.

The pay would be terrible, but he did not need the money. He was a millionaire now! Jack just needed an occupation he could tell people about, since he could not go around calling himself a professional killer. He could if he joined a criminal organization, but he worked alone and didn't really know how one got into such gangs without connections anyways. Criminal activities and killer jobs were not exactly advertised. The hours as a teacher would be much better than that of a surgeon. He could finish university earlier. Plus, he would get entire summers off. Sure, he could have the whole year off if he chose not to work at all, but he needed to be part of society. He didn't want to turn into the creepy neighbour who never went out.

Since Jack felt like he was entering a new phase in his life, he decided to part with his souvenir shoebox.

He went back into the woods where he had murdered Angela, and dug a deep hole beside a maple tree. He buried his box six feet under the ground, like a casket. He felt the need to leave a landmark, in case he ever wanted to take another peep at his amateurish work. He carved the letters J.A.C.K on the trunk. He also cut off chunks of the bark under his name, forming an arrow that pointed down towards the ground.

If anyone ever found his precious treasure, they would surely bring it to the police. But, he doubted that anyone would venture so far into the woods and think to dig by the tree.

Jack planted some purple flowers above the dirt he had disturbed to make it look like a gravesite. He remembered burying his cat in the forest after it had died, and making the burial ground nice like his adoptive parents had suggested. He reckoned that a lot of other people had buried their deceased pets within this forest, close to one of the paths.

# Chapter 2:

The saddest day of Jack's life took place when he saw big flames at a distance and realised it was his perfect house burning up.

The woman he had locked up in his basement somehow managed to break free of her ropes and lit up a few of her restaurant matches. She undressed herself, purposely set her clothes on fire and left them by the locked door, hoping that the wood would eventually burn and that the thick black smoke might alert neighbours.

She added a full can of gasoline to her pile of clothing after seeing that her matches barely did anything. Since Jack kept a lot of his nice oil paintings nearby, they nourished the fire as much as the gas did, and made the flames rapidly spread all over the house.

The woman had been trapped in the hot basement, unable to get out or scream for help. By the time she was found, she was crispy and unrecognisable. The ropes Jack had tied her with no longer existed. Her clothes, shoes, and purse were gone as well.

Jack told the firemen that the burned woman was his new girlfriend and that she had spent the night; a realistic scenario if nobody found out that she had been a prostitute. He didn't think that anybody had seen her get into his car the night before, or had taken notice of details such as his licence plate or car mark if they did see her open the passenger door and sit down inside his vehicle.

He caused a dramatic scene over her death, but was really mourning over his perfect killing ground. Jack knew that he would never find another home like this unless he became a funeral director, which he had no intention of becoming. He liked death too much and would never be able to take proper care of his clients.

Lucky for Jack, he had taken a quick look at the woman's identification cards before leaving his house this morning. He would have looked suspicious if she had to be named Jane Doe.

Her name was Sandy Miller. Jack made up a story of how they met, which nobody was interested in, and pretended to cry more sad tears for her; the only tears anyone would shed for her.

Jack was afraid that his meat freezer might be opened and examined, but the appliance was no longer capable of functioning. It was black as coal, like the rest of the remaining items inside the house. It was a good thing because he had a few questionable parts stored inside. Some meat might have passed for animal flesh, but he did not always have the time to cut everything up nicely before freezing them. Legs and arms were often tossed in.

His recent souvenir collection consisting of small human bones seemed to have burned up too, which was good in a way. But, Jack felt like he had lost a limb. He cried over his lost memories like a normal human would mourn over ruined photographs, scrapbooks and other memorabilia.

The night after the fire, Jack stayed at a nearby hotel.

He went back to the remains of his house even though he had been warned that it was dangerous. Jack needed to make sure that no evidence of his killings would be found during the next day's cleanup.

Jack managed to open his freezer and take out his leftovers. He made sure that all of his souvenir bones where nowhere to be found and took whatever was left of his weapons.

Everything he deemed suspicious was put in a garbage bag, which he planned on tossing.

He left the scene covered in dark ashes.

Jack refused the insurance money to show that he did not care about his former home and belongings. They were just stuff that could be replaced. His "girlfriend" would never breathe again…

He paid for the stranger's funeral as an act of kindness, even though he was the only one who attended.

Not realising that his house could be rebuilt, a new home was purchased downtown. Jack also bought a secluded log cabin in the woods, right by a lake.

# Chapter 3:

Jack walked the snowy street of St-Catherine, prepared for his first kill of the night. Before leaving his house, he made sure his black ski mask covered his entire face, leaving room for his eyes only. He wore coloured contacts for fun, and today his eyes were green.

He kept both hands in the pockets of his long dark winter coat, concealing a flat blade in his right. He kept his face lowered to shield himself from the cold wind. Jack studied his surroundings, searching for the perfect victim.

Along a long stretch of road, he looked behind him to see if anybody was following him. Seeing nobody, he quickly advanced towards the man in front of him and stabbed him in the left kidney. The stranger fell to the ground, looking like he had simply slipped on the icy sidewalk. As Jack continued walking, he purposely dropped a small note wrapped in cardboard.

Jack kept a normal walking pace, turned the corner and found his second victim almost instantly. He stabbed a middle-aged woman in her kidney and dropped another note as he continued on his merry way. If there had been somebody around, they would not have been able to see his contented crooked smile.

By the time far away pedestrians realised that the woman was not getting up, Jack was completely out of sight. A pool of blood had formed around the woman's still body, and a piece of brown cardboard nearby was opened to reveal a note inside it that read "just another common kill".

Jack found two more sidewalk victims that night in December, leaving his signature note behind each time. He had proudly come up with it that morning.

Nobody seemed to realise that any of the murders had taken place until they got closer to the fallen people.

Before heading home for the night, Jack found a homeless man sleeping in an alleyway and cut his kidney out. He fried it up with some green beans and ate it as a midnight snack.

Four individual calls were made to the police, reporting the strange murders.

The first caller hysterically announced that she had found a body on the sidewalk, and that blood was spreading everywhere. Not even five minutes later, a man called to announce the murder of a teenage boy. Two minutes after that, another hysterical woman called to report a lady in need of an ambulance. Of course, she did not realise that nothing could help this poor woman. Another twenty minutes went by before the fourth call came in. A teenage girl this time! By that point, police cars were already on their way to the first scene.

When Detective Smith saw the first body, he was baffled at how easy it had been for the murderer to leave the scene unnoticed.

Officer Griffin found the note left by the killer and handed it to his superior. "just another common kill", the detective read aloud. "Go see if there are similar notes around the other victims", he ordered.

Officer Griffin came back with three other cardboard wrapped notes that were wet with the snow. They all said the same thing.

By then, police had gone knocking on doors, asking if anybody had seen or heard anything. Nobody saw anything unusual, except for one of the callers.

Carl Lafleur told the police that he was looking out of his living room window when he saw a tall, heavy man of about five foot ten walk past a teenage boy. He claimed the boy simply fell to the ground. When he realised that the boy was not getting up, he began to see dark liquid flowing out of the boy's body. "At first, I thought the boy had slipped", he said. "But the blood was coming from his side and it made no sense. I got dressed and went outside to see the boy. That's when I noticed a small cut in his jacket. I could see a wound there so I called 9-1-1 right away." The officers listened to the witness's story and took down notes on the suspect's physical characteristics.

Jack had padded his extra large winter coat to make himself look overweight, so the description given was inaccurate. Since Jack had pulled his hood over his head, his only witness wasn't even able to tell the police about the skull patch he had on the top of his ski mask. He wasn't able to tell that Jack was bald either; He did not trust barbers because of a horrific English story he had heard in his past life about a revengeful barber cutting his client's throats, so he had shaved his head himself.

The police did not have much to work with. They couldn't even follow footsteps left in the snow because the rough wind had whipped them all away within seconds.

Back home, Jack pulled out his bloody knife and wiped it clean on an artist's white, five by eight small canvas. There was not much liquid to make art, but Jack still wanted a souvenir of his kills. This was his first attempt at abstract art, and he was pleased with his finished product.

He remembered having to part with his first organ trophy and cursed out loud. He temporarily got more upset by thinking about his previous collection of bones. Those were trophies that could never be replaced either.

Jack had tried to note down all the killings he had done during his adult years, but there had been too many to remember.

Now that he lived on his own and barely had any visitors any more, Jack considered building a massive collection of body parts in his basement freezer. He wouldn't grind most of the meat like before.

Jack thought about creating a human puzzle, by collecting various organs and body parts from several victims over time. That would be his masterpiece!

# Chapter 4:

The newspapers wrote about the four stabbed victims, leaving the signature notes out of the story. Police had kept been quiet about that. The papers never mentioned the homeless man Jack had disposed of inside a commercial dumpster either. Maybe Jack would give the police a hint.

Jack cut out all the articles about his recent work and tapped them inside an eight by ten spiral notebook. This was the murder journal he started after his house burned down. It didn't have a lock, but he felt like securing books that way only made them more interesting to others.

Diary locks were so easy to open. Jack had picked Sally and Abby's diaries unlocked with a sharpened pencil several times when they lived together.

Jack made a single photocopy of the most interesting article for the police and drew a picture of a dumpster in the corner. He circled the names of the four victims and made individual line pattern from each of the names all the way to his hand drawn picture. Jack marked the drawing with a big red X.

After receiving the strange photocopy, police went back to each crime scene and looked around for dumpsters. By then, the contents had already been picked up by dump trucks.

The news announced a possible fifth victim. Since nobody was reported missing, police considered the letter as a probable fluke.

A forensics team examined the "just another common kill" notes along with the mailed photocopy, but found no prints.

The cardboard was cut from four different cereal boxes. The thin notes had been written on a lined piece of paper torn from a common note pad, sold in every office supply store worldwide. The ink used wasn't from any special pen. There was no saliva on the envelope the strange paper had come in, and no return address.

All the notes were bagged and kept as evidence, but not much could be done with them.

# Chapter 5:

An eyeless body was found on Stanley Street, near one of the entrances of the Peel Metro station. Inside the right eyehole, an unwrapped "just another common kill" note was placed.

The night before, Jack wandered the busy streets of Montreal and brought home a drugged up prostitute. He tied her to his four posts bed with play handcuffs, but instead of having kinky sex with her he tortured her.

Roxanne's eyelids were being held open against her will with pointy wooden toothpicks. She was forced to watch as Jack approached a small sewing needle towards her right eye, and then the left one. After a few minutes of teasing, Jack penetrated each brown eye with several needles at a time and left them there.

Since the eyes have no pain receptors, Roxanne felt no initial pain. However, seeing the needled coming towards her eyes and not being able to close them made her scream none the less.

Jack left seven needles sticking out of Roxanne's eyes and exited the room. He came back with a hot soldering iron.

The needles were slowly taken out of Roxanne's eyes. For fun, Jack quickly advanced his needle filled hand towards Roxanne's right eye and listened to her scream. He laughed as he pulled his hand away.

Taking his new toy, Jack stuck the iron halfway into the woman's left eye, turned it off, and held it in place while it cooled down. A few minutes later, he pulled the iron out. The gooey eyeball stuck to the iron and pulled out of the socket like the cork of a wine bottle. Roxanne felt THAT pain!

Jack did the same to her other eye before forcing the woman's head into a bowl of water and letting her drown.

Detective Smith was called onto the scene. Molly Wosniack, the twenty-one year old student who had discovered the body, was still shaking when he arrived. It was not because of the cold.

His fellow officers had already questioned her, but he wanted to interrogate her himself.

Molly described how she came out of the Metro station and caught a glimpse of a body. She thought it was a homeless person at first, but then she noticed that the woman had no eyes and appeared to be dead. She did not touch the body, but ran back inside to tell the man who worked at the metro ticket booth what she had seen. It was him who had reported the murder.

The metro man, Mr. Robert Fust, was interrogated too. He had nothing to add to the story aside from the fact that he did not notice anybody unusual walking through the metal turnstiles. Copies of his surveillance tapes were given to the police.

Stanley Street exit was closed off for the day, but nosy pedestrians and metro riders still tried to go by to see what all the fuss was about.

They found out on the evening news, when the link to the previous murders was revealed.

Back at the police station, the new note was examined in hopes of finding a print, but the team was unsuccessful once again.

The video from the metro showed nothing useful. It was placed with the rest of the evidence anyways, in case it needed to be viewed again at a later date.

Pictures of the long tracks left in the snow were analysed. It was clear that they were from a winter boot and that the killer had slid his feet on the ground to form two giant prints as though they had been done by wide skis. The tracks had led towards St-Catherine Street, but had been lost among multiple other boot prints.

# Chapter 6:

Jack committed two more big murders that winter.

The first body was spotted near an ice rink beside a bloody skate and a right handed hockey stick. Both arms of the buff male had been sawed off, but only the top halves were missing. Inside his hockey skate was a "just another common kill" note. The second skate was found on the ice, inside a net, along with a black puck and other hockey equipment. It appeared that the man had been practicing moves on his own during the coldest night of January.

Jack appeared not to have been as careful about covering up his boot prints this time, but that was because he had stolen his victim's winter boots before attacking him with a knife and removing the man's skate to do more damage.

With the stolen equipment bag containing the severed limbs he wanted as well as his backpack, weapons and his own boots, Jack walked back over his old prints before creating a confusing trail that went around in circles. He walked back home wearing his own boots. His feet almost got frostbitten from the change of footwear, but Jack thought he was clever anyways.

The second body was discovered in the Old Port after a melting snowman revealed what appeared to be a frozen human in a sitting position. It turned out that the man had no legs starting at the knees. The lower halves had been removed from the rest of the body, but the feet had been placed within the snow. Jack had pinned his signature note on the inside of a striped green and yellow yarn hat, which had dropped to the side of the snowman.

In the early spring, when snow had been replaced by wet slush, Jack found another victim to leave his "just another common kill" note beside. He took the right foot of a woman who was in need of crutches. Her left leg had already been broken, so it inspired Jack to break the other before killing her and taking her right kneecap with him.

---

Detective Smith worked on all three murder cases, unsure of what kind of guy he was looking for.

After his officers followed the boot prints that started near the ice rink and led to nowhere, he looked at the only suspect description he had and realised that the footprints found near the amateur hockey player did not make any sense. If the murderer had been fat, he would also be heavy. The imprints would have gone deep into the snow where it had accumulated, but the prints found appeared to have been made by a person of average height. The killer was obviously playing with them.

The snowman scene had been trampled on for days, so there was nothing to photograph or take samples of except for the frozen victim and his props. A matching scarf had been wrapped around the snowman's neck, but the set of a hat, scarf and possibly missing mittens gave nothing away.

Jack had doodled on the broken legged lady's cast, but he left no clues.

With no leads to follow, the detective and his team were starting to get discouraged.

# Chapter 7:

In May, Jack took a two and a half hour bus trip to Ottawa.

He chose a seat in the back of the bus, beside a woman who was already sitting by a left side window. Since the small toilet area occupied the right side, no other seats were beside him.

When darkness came and most people were asleep, Jack took out a syringe and used it to put his travel neighbour to permanent sleep.

He discreetly cut off her right fingers and placed them inside a medium sized Ziploc bag. Since he had done his work over the woman's lap, it was filled with blood. He left both female hands resting in the middle of the woman's lap and covered them with her burgundy purse. The red liquid slowly made its way to the floor, but nobody noticed.

Once everyone had gotten out of the bus, Jack took his suitcase and casually left to go call a taxi.

The bus driver noticed the woman in the back and walked up the aisle to go wake her up. As she wasn't responding to his "Miss, we have arrived in Ottawa", he placed his hand on her shoulder and shook her lightly. Her head remained tilted on the window. The bus driver then noticed the red formation. He lifted the woman's purse to find her mutilated hand. Her left one held a folded note.

When the Ottawa police unfolded the bloody piece of paper found by the traumatized bus driver, they saw the words "just another common kill" written on the once white page. By then, Jack was sitting in his hotel suite, drinking whiskey and smoking cheap cigars.

Jack read about the unusual case in the morning's paper. According to the front page article, the only clue left behind was a pair of black gloves, most likely belonging to a man.

Passengers coming from the eight o'clock Montreal bus were encouraged to call the police and give their names and approximate seat location on the bus. "If anyone remembers the man or woman sitting in the back seat, they are asked to please come into the station to help a sketch artist draw the suspect's face."

Jack had paid his ticket in cash and gave a false name to the ticket seller. He chose the name of a character from an unpopular horror movie.

They never asked for identification when traveling by bus within the same country. Quebec had often joked about not being part of the rest of Canada because there were a lot of separatists who wished that the province of Quebec became its own country, but it was still a part of Canada. No passports were required to travel from one province to the next unless one was flying.

Jack knew for a fact that even if everyone on that bus came forward, they would never narrow the list down to him. All they would have is a fake lead. To throw suspicion off him even more, Jack brought a long hair wig and hippy clothes for his return home, so nobody would make the connection between this peace-loving character and the business man they might have seen on the bus days before. He was starting to get good at this and taking more unnecessary risks.

# Chapter 8:

Jack ate lunch in the outside courtyard of downtown Ottawa. There, he discovered that some hangings had taken place at the very spot where he had ordered his fancy food. That gave him an idea.

That night, he offered a homeless man some free food and took him to the same courtyard. It was completely deserted, as Jack expected it would be.

Jack killed him and took his intestines out. After cutting a small chunk for himself, he formed a tight noose with them and hung the man from a strong budding tree.

Jack heard the piercing scream of a woman in the morning. He figured that the body had just been found and looked out of his hotel window. He could see everything perfectly.

He could not hear what was being said, but watching the crowd form while police tried to push everyone away was entertaining enough for him. Yellow crime tape was placed around the murder scene, which made people even more curious.

As Jack observed the commotion below him, he realised that he had not left a signature note behind. If he had a balcony, he would be able to sneak out right before check out time and let a piece of paper fall weightlessly to the ground from the third floor. Unfortunately, that was not a possibility. He pondered on whether he should just leave it alone or make his way into the frantic crowd.

Finally, he put on his hippy costume and headed downstairs. He casually walked towards the crime scene and acted like everyone else. Pretending to have to tie his shoe, he bent down and took his folded note out of his sneaker. Acting like he had picked it up from the ground, Jack unfolded it and then pushed everyone out of the way so that he could give it to the police.

"Let me pass, I found evidence on the ground!" he shouted. The nearest officer came to see him. Jack handed him the note and pointed towards where he had been standing a few seconds ago. "I thought it was garbage, but I opened it up and figured you might want it", he lied. Officer Nick thanked him and walked towards the other officers.

Seeing nothing interesting going on anymore, Jack wanted to leave. He stayed a few minutes longer in case he needed to be questioned. It might be considered suspicious behaviour if he suddenly left. If he was spotted at the bus station in this same outfit and asked for identification he would be in serious trouble. He had to stop playing with fire, even if it was part of his fun.

# Chapter 9:

Having had a bit too much to drink, Jack broke a man's nose during a bar fight.

He was arrested and brought to the Montreal police station. There, he saw that there were notes on the "just another common kill" case. He did not have the chance to read the theories, but he obviously did not fit the profile they were searching for because they let him go shortly afterwards. The guy he beat up was also brought in. Since he threw the first punch, Jack was able to get off with self-defence.

He was still finger printed for the police records. Jack took a mental note to be extra careful not to leave any prints anywhere or he would be caught right away. He cursed the evolution of forensics.

Back in 1888, he did not have to worry about leaving prints or DNA behind. It was easy to get away with any type of crime. The guilty walked the streets while innocent people were locked up. Nowadays, you had to do extra planning and think everything through. It was thrilling in a way because it made things challenging, but it took away some of the fun. You couldn't really be as spontaneous.

As revenge for putting him in the criminal system and making him more vulnerable, Jack found his bar friend and followed him home.

A few days later, he broke into the man's house and threw a live black widow at him. The angry spider bit the surprised man, poisoning him.

Jack would not let the man leave his house to go to the hospital. He waited until the man died and left the house with his ugly eight-legged friend.

He returned the creature to the Insectarium before its absence could be noticed. Being a volunteer there made it easy to steal the dangerous arachnid.

Yes, Jack could have killed his new enemy himself. But, he was sure that whatever he did would lead back to him.

If he left a "just another common kill" note behind to make it look unrelated to the bar fight, his murder days might end in a heartbeat. All it took was for one smart person to make the connection and search his house. He didn't want any attention given to this murder. He didn't even collect anything interesting for his project; just a boring fingernail clipping.

His victim obviously did cocaine. Why else would he keep his right baby fingernail that long when all the rest were nicely trimmed?

For days, Jack quickly scanned the pages of his morning paper to see if his recent victim's body had been written about. It took weeks for a three paragraph article to appear.

The body was found by the drug dealer's girlfriend. She thought it odd that he stopped returning her calls or responding to her e-mails after being in a serious relationship for close to three years. She drove to his house with the intention of using her key to get in if he did not answer. The door was unlocked, so she let herself in and tried to find her boyfriend. She noticed a bad smell and found him decomposing.

An autopsy report concluded that the man had actually died from an unusual spider poisoning, and went on to describe the effects of deadly spiders.

Jack imagined a new wave of arachnophobia being born. He was never a big fan of the creatures himself. If he had access to a reptile farm, he would have stolen a venomous snake to do his deed instead.

# Chapter 10:

Jack called a male escort and broke his jaw.

He used the name of another horror movie character when asked for his own. He was told he could pay cash if he gave the money to his escort in advance. Major credit cards were also accepted, but Jack preferred the first method of payment.

Once the two supposedly homosexual men met, Jack forced his date into his car and drove off towards his house. There, Jack temporarily taped his new friend's mouth shut with electrical tape and shoved rock salt up the guy's nose. He broke the man's fragile nose, causing him to snort the rock salt like cocaine. His nose started bleeding heavily from the damage.

When the man was dead, Jack removed the tape and disposed of it. He took the large plastic garbage bag with him when he placed the man's body in his car.

Before doing that, he cut the man's jaw off, letting his long tongue hang loose. He stored his new trophy in his freezer before leaving.

So far, his human puzzle was turning out great.

Jack found a deserted alleyway to dump the body and threw out his garbage a few blocks away. He left his "just another common kill" note rolled up inside the man's throat.

# Chapter 11:

Jack drove past an empty construction site and decided to make it his new playground.

He found a homeless man stupid enough to have a few drinks with him on the unfinished fourteenth floor. Once Jack got bored with the man's drunken company, he pushed him off the balcony and watched him hit the pavement below.

Jack left the man's bottle of liquor where they had consumed the liquid and left with his own.

He wasn't even going to bother taking a souvenir with him because he didn't know what he could take without it looking like the man was murdered instead of his death being an accident. He had his share of hair in the past and had no use for nails.

At the last minute, he saw the man's woollen scarf wrapped around the man's neck and took it. He could accessorize his human puzzle like children did to snowmen.

A few weeks later, Jack left for a boat cruise down south.

He remembered how interesting it had been to watch a man fall from fourteen floors and wondered if pushing a guy from the ship's highest floor's railing would have the same effect.

Each night, Jack stood on the tenth floor of the ship and waited to find somebody looking over the high railing.

On his last day, a man was star watching. Jack cut the man with his knife and stole his hat before pushing him overboard. He watched as the stranger fell and hit the water.

Jack concluded that it had the same damaging affect as landing on cement. The man most likely died on impact; lucky for him because hungry sharks tore the man apart moments later.

# Chapter 12:

Jack captured a man and locked him in place with the set of balls and chains he owned. Although the confused man could move his legs if he forced himself, Jack used his leather whip on the man's bare back every time he tried.

The man attempted to escape the basement when Jack left him down there by himself, but his kidnapper came back once he reached the stairs. Jack pinned the guy's arms to the wall using long nails. He then taped the man's mouth shut with duct tape.

Earlier, a neighbour had heard the screams of a man coming from an open window and had come to the door to investigate. Jack laughed and told him he was watching a horror movie, but appreciated his concern. He was mad at himself for almost getting caught. He really missed his old home.

As a punishment to the man for almost giving away his position, Jack went back upstairs and came back with some plain paper. He tore the duct tape off and made several paper cuts to the man's tongue and lips. He cut off a fresh piece of tape after and placed it over the man's bleeding mouth.

He left him there to starve.

When the man was finally dead, Jack cut him up into pieces and stored the divided parts of meat in his freezer. It was taking too long to collect parts for his puzzle so Jack was collecting bigger pieces now. More was taken from his victims.

Jack considered buying another house so that he could keep his living space and torture areas separate. His cottage was too far away. Instead, he rented an apartment to live in, and kept his house for his personal amusement. He now kept his windows closed at all times.

He bought new furniture and paintings for his apartment, making it nice and cozy looking. He even bought a few tall plants to decorate, even if he was far from having green thumbs. The only vegetal life form he was ever able to keep alive was a cactus. Nevertheless, Jack made an effort to look normal. At a glance, nobody would ever suspect he had a dark side. He was just a typical bachelor.

He hung several replica paintings of nude women, originally done by Walter Sickert in his bedroom. It was his personal joke.

Jack's house was redecorated to his tastes. His torture weapons remained on display in the basement, and his freezer full of human body parts was kept in the corner. He painted all the walls maroon and took the time to hang some of his morbid paintings and drawings. He never entertained guests he did not intend on killing there.

# Chapter 13:

Over the course of the year, Jack experimented with all of his medieval torture devices, and imported many new ones into the country.

He had managed to acquire a guillotine, solid wooden stocks in which he could lock his victims up uncomfortably for hours and throw large stones directly at their trapped heads and hands, a full head mask that enabled the one wearing it to speak because of the long metal bit jamming deep into the mouth, heavy iron boots in which hot oil could be poured while his victim was wearing them, a neck brace with pointy interior spikes, a lead sprinkler in which boiling water was splashed onto his victims, a Spanish tickler used to rip the flesh right off the bones, and an inquisition chair in which he would violently push his naked victims onto the spiked seat.

Sometimes, Jack would heat up his special chair when his victim was strapped in, and let the metal cook his victim's bare flesh. The smell never bothered him, but it always traumatised the one in the chair.

He made his victims cry out with both fear and pain with his Iron Maiden, a cabinet full of interior spikes. Once the door was shut, the randomly spaced out spikes jammed themselves into the trapped victim. Jack would slam the door and let his victims bleed for a day, then change their position from standing with their backs turned to the door to having them face the hellish spikes. He kept them alive and in agony for days.

Jack's favourite toy was his rack, because he could easily dislocate every single joint of the body by pulling the legs and arms of his victim in opposite directions, farther than it was physically possible.

Jack also owned a chastity belt with an old style key and had forced a prostitute to put it on before letting her back on the streets. For fun, he had sent her on a pointless treasure hunt in search of the key. He wondered how long the woman had followed his clues before finding the melted remains of the now useless key.

He bought manacles, a finger trap, thumbscrews, a tongue tearer, a breast ripper, a knee splitter, a head crusher, a rusted cage, heavy chains...

Jack came up with more inventive ways to play and dismember his victims to make his desired puzzle. Once, he played darts using the target he had painted on his male victim's bare chest. He finished the man off with his bow and arrows.

He had a large assortment of weapons too now. Jack had several swords, different sizes of daggers, throwing stars, double-sided and single-sided axes, a morning star...

Sometimes, Jack would become a little bit creative and use his modern tools, such as hammers and screwdrivers, to play with his victims. He created his own torture devices and murder weapons.

Jack was getting really good at luring his victims into his murder home or deserted alleyways. His only flaw was that he was starting to get too impatient and almost got caught dumping remains several times.

He didn't always leave bodies to be found because it became too risky. He preferred to leave occasional notes when he felt it safe to place incomplete bodies somewhere, but he mostly just bagged up what he didn't need and tossed them in garbage bins that were not his own or in public dumpsters.

His murders became less talked about because the news started announcing more missing people than actual bodies found. Jack didn't mind. He needed people to start forgetting about the "just another common kill" notes for a while so that he could continue working near his home.

Jack wanted to leave one disturbing mess with his final note and have his grand artwork become popular for more than just a few weeks. He wanted to be remembered for something original.

He needed to be far away from civilization, but only had weekends to escape.

# Chapter 14:

Jack turned a man into a human torch by pouring gasoline on him and throwing a lit match towards the innocent hitchhiker. He planned on eating as much as his stomach would allow him to, but found that the barbecued meat was overcooked.

He didn't think that his new pets, two baby Amazon piranhas, would enjoy the meat either. They had not yet been picky about the food Jack dropped in their heated aquarium, but he felt that they deserved the best. They ate nothing that Jack wouldn't put in his own mouth and swallow.

Disappointed, Jack left the burned man on the side of the deserted highway and drove to a diner. There, he ordered the lunch special. They were serving ribs, his favourite non-cannibalistic meal.

After his light meal, Jack continued driving towards his cabin. He needed to figure out what he was doing.

He picked up another hitchhiker and brought the man deep into the woods. He told the man to run as fast as he could while he took out his loaded hunting riffle, the only gun he ever owned.

The frightened man took Jack seriously right away, but did not have time to run far enough. Jack shot him in the back and walked towards his wounded prey. He finished him off by shooting him directly in the heart, and dragged the man back to his car.

Jack did not stop at the general store for food as he usually did. He had just hunted enough meat for the weekend.

Wouldn't it be funny if he put up his victim's head on display on top of his fireplace like prideful hunters did with deer heads? Jack agreed with himself, but kept the man's head for his purple instead. Since he already had a jaw, he only took the top half of the head.

His cabin was a much better place to saw off body parts. He could use his chainsaw without any neighbours complaining about the sound.

# Chapter 15:

Jack wasn't able to collect enough body parts to make his desired puzzle because he had midnight cravings for human meat and ate most of what he collected.

He also continued to share his meat with his piranhas. They had become good partners with him by devouring most of what Jack originally had to toss. After they were done their meals, only clean bones were left.

Although Jack had saved entire bodies to satisfy his large appetite and that of his carnivorous fishes, he just ended up wanting more once he had consumed all the human meat he had. Jack no longer ate anything else from the other food groups; just meat.

Most of his victims became food instead of artwork.

Jack's skin had developed a yellow tint because of all his human meat consumption, but nobody took much notice. The change had started occurring during his medical studies, once his cannibalistic acts became part of his weekly diet.

# Part 3

## (Fun old games)

# Chapter 1:

A year and a half had gone by since Jack left his last "just another common kill" note behind.

Jack decided to play a fun game, based on his previous intentions.

As a biology and chemistry high school teacher, he had the entire summer off to do whatever he pleased. He packed a suitcase full of normal everyday clothes and ordinary disguises for the long road trip he was about to go on.

His plan was to hit every single state of his neighbouring country, except for Hawaii and Alaska, and commit at least one brutal murder in each one. He strategically mapped out a basic traveling plan, figuring out the order each state would be visited.

Before leaving, Jack wrote two notes using his computer. One was actually a short letter and the others were simply a revised version of his old signature note. Jack used several creepy looking fonts for both the letter and his note so that he would have different versions of each one of them.

Jack printed out dozens of copies of his styled letters and signature notes using red lettering, stuck each paper in individual envelopes, sealed them with clear double sided tape and placed them all inside a brand new briefcase.

This novelty had been purchased using cash, to eliminate the possibility of such a case ever being owned by him if it were found with the sealed envelopes still inside. Jack distrusted credit card companies when it came to buying things for his murder games. Everything was noted on invoices and he didn't like it.

Jack also distrusted his computer. He knew that even if he deleted something, the computer still kept it in its memory somewhere and everything could somehow be retrieved. In case his house was ever searched, Jack destroyed his computer and tossed it in the garbage. He could buy another one when he got back.

To be extra safe, Jack had used thin gloves to take the white pages out of their plastic wrapper before inserting them into his laser printer, and wore them to open up his boxes of envelopes as well. He used small envelopes for the signature notes, and larger ones for the letters he planned on mailing. He tossed all the leftover envelopes, taking a mental note not to buy the same ones again.

Jack brought his murder journal with him, as well as a digital camera with a memory card and extra AA batteries. Jack made sure to pack several large Ziploc bags, plastic wrappings, disposable gloves as well as his collection of sharp blades and surgical tools. He brought a few small medieval items with him as well.

In the state of Maine, Jack killed a careless jaywalker too focused on his blasting rap music to notice the approaching car. Jack pushed the gas pedal, hit the man hard, ran over him and his mega earphones, backed up on the body and came out of his car to collect his road kill.

He sent the man's toeless feet to the local newspapers. A note was placed inside the parcel. It read:

*"Dear audience,*
*Here is a piece of my special puzzle.*
*I would have written my note in fresh blood, but knew that I would not have the time. I hope my red ink is good enough for you. Ha,ha.*
*I am going to enjoy playing this little game because I love my work.*
*Please keep this puzzle piece until I have sent out all the others.*
*Yours truly,*
*Just another common killer"*

He left the state the next morning after taking a copy of the newspaper with him. His work had already made local headlines.

He drove to New Hampshire, where he scalped a man in his thirties and sent the hairy piece of flesh to another newspaper. The same note was placed inside. At first, the scalp was mistaken by reporters for a wig, but the dry blood below the black mass made them realise that it was the top of a human's head.

The body it belonged to was found hours later with Jack's new signature note "Just another common killer". This was another hit for the media!

Upon reaching Massachusetts, Jack kidnapped a male child around the age of nine, but was unable to do him any harm. Killing kids had been different when he was a youth himself. Now he just couldn't do it.

He let the boy go after taking samples of his toenails, but told him he would come back for him if he ever told anybody about his existence.

As boring as he felt his new catch was, he sent it to the press anyways. He didn't bother sending a letter with it, and nothing was mentioned in the papers.

In Vermont, Jack collected five ugly toes (two from the left foot and three from the right) from a man in serious need of a pedicure. He ripped the thick yellowish toenails right off before mailing the fat limbs along with a letter.

In Rhode Island, Jack beheaded a drunken young adult and took his brain out. He left the man's severed head with the body and mailed the brain.

He mailed a different brainless head in Connecticut. Only the top part was sent, but without the eyes, eyelids, nose, or scalp.

New York brought Jack to Central Park, where he found a happy couple making out on a vandalized bench. He cut off both their tongues and sent half of each to the press. He ate the other halves raw.

In New Jersey, Jack broke the jaw of a random female pedestrian and parcelled the fleshy bone, complete with perfect lower teeth.

Jack visited the White House in D.C. and left a discrete little present behind; an eyeball. He hid it inside the pot of a giant plant during a guided tour.

In Delaware, Jack mailed a man's nose.

The Maryland press was given an unhealthy liver. The victim had been waiting for an organ transplant, but Jack stole the replacement liver for his dinner.

A young female student in Pennsylvania lost eight fingers to Jack. He loved the fact that she had painted all her long fingernails bright red.

In Virginia, Jack mailed a woman's folded right arm, leaving out the hand. He mailed a man's handless left arm in West Virginia.

In North Carolina, he mailed a man's footless right leg, and he mailed a woman's left leg in South Carolina. Both times, only the bottom halves were sent.

In Georgia he sent the top half of a woman's leg, including the knee, and in Florida he sent the top half of a man's knee-less leg.

The Alabama press received the beating heart of a tuna fish. Jack remembered from his biology studies and previous dissection labs that hearts continued to pulse until all the blood was out of that muscle. After being detached from the rest of the bodies, hearts lived on. The bigger the heart was, the longer it took to stop beating, but fish hearts were easier to keep alive because they were less complex. So, Jack thought it would be a fun present to send if it made it to its destination on time. The freaky, hand delivered parcel, marked urgent, made a great story; especially after a human heart was received with Jack's playful letter a few hours later.

Jack collected a knee in Mississippi.

In Tennessee, Jack sent a bag of gooey guts to the press.

He mailed human ribs covered in sticky barbeque sauce to the Kentucky newspapers.

Ohio received a fingerless left hand. Michigan received a fingerless right hand.

In Indiana, Jack stole a right thumb from a homeless man. He took a left one from a woman in Illinois.

Jack wrapped up intestines like a snake before sending it off to the Wisconsin press.

In Iowa, Jack collected five more toes; they were from a woman's feet this time. Three were from her petite left foot and two were taken from the right.

Jack collected soft female skin in Missouri. The pinkish leather was taken from her chubby back.

In Arkansas, Jack packaged a man's precious genitals. He did the same with a woman's reproductive system in Louisiana.

In Texas, Jack removed the thin eyelids from a blind man. He sent them along with the attached black lashes. His signature note was included. Jack kept this victim alive, but had instructed the man to make his way to the press building Jack had given him the address to, and hand over an envelope containing his letter. To ensure that the man would complete his task, he had written the address on the envelope and had given him more than enough money to take a cab. He had even called a taxi company from a payphone before deserting him.

Jack severed a woman's head in Oklahoma. He sent off her neck, with the top and bottom bones sticking out.

When Jack got to Kansas, he spotted a good-looking woman with piercing blue eyes and took her left one out. Her found another attractive woman in Nebraska and took her lovely right green eye.

Jack collected two shoulder blades from soup kitchen volunteers in South Dakota. He completely removed all the muscles and nerves from them, and sent the bare bones to the press. He donated all the human meat he was able to collect to the same soup kitchen.

In Wyoming, Jack cut off the thin glossy lips from a woman.

Jack took a man's kidney in Colorado.

In New Mexico, Jack filled one of his smaller Ziploc bags with blood and placed it in a bigger one before mailing the liquid.

Jack made a quick stop in the country of Mexico. There, he murdered the first Mexican he saw and left his signature note behind. Nothing was mailed. He simply bought a postcard and left the hot country.

In Arizona, Jack bagged a pound of pure human fat.

In Utah, he stood in front of an abortion clinic and kidnapped the first pregnant woman he saw. He messily took her baby out, and left her alive. She bled to death in the alleyway Jack performed his messy operation in.

The small male foetus was Ziploced and mailed to an orphanage. Jack was upset at not reading about it in the next morning's paper. He would have to wait until he got home and search the Internet for his news article. Hopefully, there would be something written about his present by the time he got back to Canada.

A showgirl was killed in Nevada. Jack cut her big breasts, only to find out the they weren't real. He mailed the detached nipples with some of the silicone.

A want-to-be actress in California was lured by Jack pretending to be a film director. Her blackened lungs were taken from her.

In Oregon, Jack collected several worm-looking veins.

Jack took a man's stomach in Washington.

In Idaho, Jack removed the tight abdomen of a muscular man.

Jack sent away an incomplete backbone in Montana.

In North Dakota, Jack took a pancreas.

Jack killed his last U.S victim in Minnesota. He cut out a main artery and sent it away.

Each time Jack selected a victim, he took a picture of his finished work and left a "Just another common killer" note behind. He would bag whatever body part suited him, bring it to his hotel, take a picture of it, package it, and mail it to the local press (or other building he thought fitting), along with his special letter. He owned a fancy envelope labeller so he used it to write up the addresses he needed and stuck the printed stickers onto his large envelopes.

He always stayed in a city long enough to get articles on his work and quickly moved on to the next state. When the cheap hotels he stayed in had guest books, he always wrote a comment about his murder, doodled, or signed his killer name on top of already filled pages.

When he got back to Canada, he printed his pictures from his new home computer and sent random copies to half of the newspapers he had written to during his stay in the United States of America. With it, a list of all the body parts he sent out along with the states he had taken them from was included. At the bottom of the list, he wrote *The puzzle is still missing pieces, but this is the best I could do. Have fun building your hermaphrodite. Just another common killer."*

The news of his murders and parcels spread like a bad rumour. Jack was content with his secret fame.

Since he did not want to disappoint his new audience, he found one last victim and sent her insides to the White House with a note. *"Here are more pieces to the human puzzle. I hope the other parts are still intact. Just another common killer"*


Because the last two letters had been mailed from Canada rather than the US, police from both countries started working together.

The "just another common kill" murders were brought up again. Profilers were trying to decide if both sets of murders were done by the same person, or if the second set was simply influenced by the first.

It seemed like they were unrelated because the "just another common kill" notes had been written in fresh ink while the "Just another common killer" notes were all typed. Plus, the first alphabet letter of all the "just another common kill" notes were never capitalized while it always was on the second set of notes and letters. Nothing was ever mailed during the first set of murders, but the killer could have evolved. It was unlikely that the killer would have gone from killing in the same area to spreading out his murders outside of his comfort zone though. It was clear that whoever the murderer of the second series was liked to travel. It was brought up that there had been two "just another common kill" notes left in the capital city of Canada rather than in Montreal like the majority of them, but the distance became insignificant compared to the travels the second set of murders necessitated.

The Mexican murder was finally linked after Jack sent his Mexican postcard to the Canadian authorities with the words "just another common kill" printed on the back. This settled their non-publicized uncertainty about the "just another common kill" notes and the "Just another common killer" notes being from the same person.

Jack pondered on his next game and came up with several amusing murder plans. But, he decided he would wait until his latest fame died down before starting his new murder series. In the meantime, he amused himself by doodling pictures of his recent set of murders. He also collected a significant amount of newspaper clippings and articles about himself he found on the Internet.

He ended up making a large collage of article copies and drawings, which he turned into a giant puzzle. Before cutting up his artwork into miniscule pieces, he painted his name with maroon paint, right in the centre. Maybe he would send it to the police one day. He didn't think that the officers would spend their time doing his impossible puzzle any more than they would have tried to put together all the human body parts he had sent out.

Jack loved reading about the different theories on him. Some profilers thought he might be a butcher because of the way he cut up the bodies so cleanly, others believed he was a doctor because of his knowledge of the human anatomy. Most journalists simply described him as a sick lunatic. Jack did not like that insinuation. He noticed the occasional references to Jack the Ripper since most of the bodies found were those of prostitutes, strippers, escorts, erotic massage therapists and sex shop employees. Plus, his repeated letter was eventually analysed by experts who noticed that it was very similar to the old killer's way of writing. Some said he might be a psychotic fan trying to become a murder legend in his own creative way. His morbid idea of trying to create a human puzzle lead some to believe that he could be a crazy artist; a lot if artistic people had been known to be slightly deranged. Thoughts about him being sexually dysfunctional or perhaps being born with both female and male organs were mentioned.

Whatever he was, Hollywood became interested in doing their version of Jack's story and started working on a horror flick.

# Chapter 2:

Jack sat in the back of the filled movie theatre, wondering why people generally got disturbed by horrific tales told on the evening news, but paid money to watch people get tortured and murdered on the big screen as a form of entertainment. The gorier the better!

It made him think about all the torture devices he had back home.

Murder has always been considered a sin, but years ago killing a criminal by means of beheading, hanging, burning, inflicting pain, or leaving them to die of starvation was a public punishment. Crowds would gather to watch, cheer and sometimes participate in the punishment act. Children were included.

If people liked this form of entertainment, Jack wondered, why is it illegal to kill or torture? Should he reconsider his choice of victims and only select other criminals? Is that what makes it ok in the eyes of society?

The thought of having to carefully select his victims, just like the main character of his favourite television series, instead of choosing at random suddenly took the fun out of killing. But, pre-setting specific characteristics might add a little something to his favourite game. It might make it more challenging.

Jack was taken away from his daydream when the movie finally started. He put on his stupid looking 3D glasses like the rest of the audience did.

The theatre fell silent, but the scream of several women broke the quiet room as an unexpected shadow moved across the screen and a three-dimensional knife moved into the audience. The title "Just Another Common Killer" was written in bloody dripping letters. Jack liked how each word was capitalized, forming his birth name JACK.

The name of the main character was, of course, Jack. The ones who came up with that must think them selves so smart, Jack thought to himself. It had taken Jack weeks to make something interesting up using the letters of his name as a teasing signature. He wondered how hard it had been for movie writers to try and find a human name for "Just another common killer". Did they excitingly yell out "I got it!" and share the information the same way Jack would have liked to do?

Halfway through the 3D movie, Jack became bored. He much preferred live performances. This audience was scared, but were not panicked because they still felt safe in their seats. Jack could hear them sipping soda through their straws, picking out candies from plastic bags, and munching on popcorn.

The typical scary "something is about to happen" music started. Some people whispered amongst each other. Most females let out screams here and there while their macho male companions laughed at them.

When the killer on the screen made his move to the sound of the loud expressive music, Jack took out a fountain pen and stabbed the man in front of him right in the throat. The surprised stranger instantly started coughing up blood. People actually shushed him when he got up and tried to ask for help. Jack laughed silently and left the theatre, pretending to simply need to go to the bathroom.

Jack disposed his not-too-bloody gloves in the men's room garbage and re-entered the theatre a few minutes later. A small crowd had gathered around the wounded man. The movie had been stopped and all the lights were back on. Nobody was allowed to leave. Jack however, was told to exit by a security guard. Jack was not too upset. He had seen what he needed.

# Chapter 3:

On the night of April 3, an old looking Jack sat alone at the bar. He had shown up in his costume at this particular bar several times this month.

Tonight, a rather drunk brunette sat down close by and told everyone that if they wanted a good time to just ask for Emma.

The thirty year old woman was dressed in a tight black tank top covering a push up bra, a red leather miniskirt and matching knee high stiletto boots. The long coat she was loosely holding fell to the ground.

Jack hoped that other men would ignore her and that she would leave the bar alone because she was perfect for the new game he wanted play. Shortly before closing time, Emma stumbled out of the bar.

Jack left a few minutes later. He discreetly followed Emma down the street. It was not hard to catch up to her since he was a very fast walker, and Emma's drunken nature and footwear slowed her down.

When Jack was close enough, he hit her in the head several times. He took all the money she had in her purse; there was a grand total of eight hundred dollars in bills of tens and twenties. Somebody had been working hard tonight, he thought to himself.

After placing his new fortune in his wallet and placing it back in his coat pocket, he started cutting Emma's stomach open. He got scared when he heard a car coming. How could he have been so stupid to try performing a dissection out in the open like that? He usually did his kills quickly and discreetly when they were done in public, or took the time to attack near or inside an alleyway so he could have some privacy afterwards.

Back in 1888, there was a slaughterhouse around his favourite killing area (Whitechapel), so it was not uncommon to see people with some blood on them. Men and women often had no choice but to walk in the bloody and gut infested streets near the slaughterhouse. Back then, nobody could tell the difference between animal blood and human blood. He had never been too afraid of being seen with a bit of red liquid on his person. Now he was.

He could not leave his bloody clothes somewhere because, if found, they would be analyzed for possible DNA. It was not as easy to remove a layer and carry it someplace far from the crime scene but not too close to his house. He had several hideouts before and they had all been too simple to rent out un-questioned while wearing a disguise. Now, pieces of identification and credit checks were done!

There was no use trying to run away at the present time. With the police car in plain view and approaching too fast for him to go anywhere unnoticed, he would look highly suspicious. Instead, he flagged the approaching car and asked the two officers to call an ambulance.

Jack told the men that he had been walking home, as he often took night strolls when he could not sleep, and heard a woman scream. He would have run if he had been in shape, but could only walk as fast as his old tired legs would allow him.

When he arrived at this location, he saw the woman lying on the ground and kneeled down beside her. He did not own a cell phone. By the time he re-alised that he was full of her blood, he noticed a car and thought they could help.

Indeed the officers were able to call an emergency vehicle. Jack heard the sirens approaching and die in front of Emma's bleeding body. The blue and red lights stayed on.

Jack was afraid that Emma might survive her attack and manage to tell the officers who had cut her up. Jack was wearing a realistic enough disguise to fool anybody, but he still wished that he would of had the time to take it off and dispose of it before the police car arrived. If she spoke, she would describe Jack exactly how he was now and his game would be over before it had really begun.

It wouldn't matter that he had managed to slide his knife inside an open sewer before getting up to flag the police, or that his figure appeared too weak to attack anyone. The illusion he created would soon fade.

The ambulance left with Emma. It was not as fun to watch this modern vehicle bring his victim away. Heavy hand-drawn carts were the ambulances back in the good old killing days. People had to really use their strength to get it moving forward and everyone saw what was inside. Now, he didn't know what was going on. Jack became nervous and prayed that Emma would not survive.

Naturally, Jack was brought to the police station for questioning. He hoped that they would not examine him too closely because they might notice his well-made disguise. He could not take his hat or gloves off or his youth would be revealed, so he pretended to be colder than he really was.

Fortunately, Jack was let go after an hour of general questioning. Aside from the blood found on Jack, which could be explained, there was not any ev-idence to make an arrest.

His wallet had not been checked, so they did not ask him about the unusual amount of money it held or the cards belonging to a much younger man not matching the name he had given his interviewers.

Jack was let go. Since he hadn't been finger printed, he would never become suspicious or linked to this murder after tonight.

Jack was told to give his number and address. Jack gave them false information. When the police dropped him at his supposed house, he went straight to the back and remained in the yard until he was sure that the police car had left the area.

He took his disguise off and dumped it in the garbage bin he found beside the barbeque. He moved the garbage around so that his wig and fake skin would end up at the very bottom. He then climbed a metal fence so that he could walk on a different street. He almost got bitten by the guard dog, but made it out of the yard unharmed.

The next morning, Jack read that a prostitute by the name of Emma Madison had been rushed to the hospital because she was found with severe head wounds and a slightly cut up stomach. She died of internal bleeding, and the baby girl she was carrying died with her.

There had been several cases of unsuccessful street abortions in the last few months; mostly teenage girls who wanted to avoid their operations being discovered and not having the money to pay for one without having to show her health card. Authorities came to the conclusion that Emma had requested an illegal abortion and changed her mind after the operation had already started. She may have run away from her illegal abortionist, who chased her and managed to kill her so that she would not reveal his messy work to anyone.

Jack could not believe how close he had gotten to being caught. It was so easy to get away with murder back in 1888!

His close call did not made Jack give up his plan though. He intended on doing his next kill in four months. He would have time to prepare more carefully. He needed to think with his modern mind and listen to his instincts rather than act upon his past life impulses.

# Chapter 4:

On August 5, Jack called an escort agency and asked for Martha. That agency had no girls by the name of Martha, so Jack told the woman on the other end that he must have the wrong number.

The following agency he called told him he could see a list of names and physical description of all the call girls on their website. Jack browsed the Internet and found several names of interest. He did not care so much about the looks of the girls.

Jack phoned the second agency again and asked that Martha the fiery red head accompany him to see a show. He gave the false name Ed Hide based on his favourite fictional character Edward Hyde, and requested that the escort meet him inside the Bell Centre, right by the gift shop.

The following evening, Jack met Martha in the crowd. She was not hard to miss. They went to their assigned seats and watched the jazz concert together. Between intermission and the end of the show, Jack asked Martha if they could be alone. For an extra hundred dollars to the original fee, Martha accepted.

The couple left towards the staircase.

Jack did not give Martha the time to perform the sexual favours he originally asked for, even though this woman would not have to ask where his penis was like Martha Tabram had back in 1888.

Jack remembered the surgeries he had undergone as a child because of his deformed and almost inexistent organ, and it brought on the same anger in the present as it had in the past.

Although he had been a very handsome man, he had lacked an important limb, which brought on ridicule and shame. He hated woman back then for making fun of him in his adult life, and despised his mother for letting his father degrade him as a child. It had been bad enough that he was brought from Germany to England for the painful operation and could not understand what the nurses or doctors were telling him or why his sensitive limb was being cut. His parents referred to him and his brothers as Walter and the boys, as though he was a sex apart.

Angry, Jack stabbed Martha Sigma in random places and left her at the bottom of the staircase, where she would be found in a pool of blood matching her flashy hair colour shortly afterwards.

Jack learned from his past life not to stab a person too many times, or he would be covered in blood and not be able to evade suspicion. The darkness and fog had saved him from his 1888 mistake.

Jack was prepared to cut himself at the side and pretend to have been attacked as well if necessary. But, he preferred not to harm himself.

He only used one weapon this time, rather than two, because security was tight. He used his beloved dagger stick, disguised as a cane. Jack would walk out of the crowded area just like he had come in; with a limp.

Of course, there would be too many people walking around to make any arrests by the time Martha was found.

Jack could not be tracked because he was careful to use a payphone when he had called the agency, just like he had done during his experimental play days. He hoped his conversation had not been recorded, but had used a voice changer just in case. It was too obvious to use again because it sounded like he had a voice box, but if it did not get mentioned in the papers he would be safe to call the same agency and talk in his normal voice next time.

# Chapter 5:

On August 31, Jack spotted a lonely young woman at a pub and asked if he could sit down with her. She accepted.

Since she would not give him her name, Jack introduced himself as Henry Jekyll, his other favourite fictional character, and he called her Polly. She found the name funny because it reminded her of a parrot. Because the girl kept saying: "Polly want a cracker?" in an irritating voice, Jack changed her name to Mary Ann. She made a comment about that too, so he just called her Mary. She thought the simplified name sounded too holy and went on and on about how she was no angel. Finally, Jack bluntly asked if he could take her home.

Mary and Jack left the pub together and headed towards Mary's place. Jack liked that idea better because he wouldn't have to clean the mess he was about to make.

Even though Mary already had too much to drink, she took out a bottle of Baileys and poured herself a glass over ice cubes. She asked Jack if he wanted some too, but he declined. He just wanted to get to work.

Mary eventually took Jack in her bedroom. They savagely had sex. Jack got upset at himself for not being able to hide his knife anywhere close by when they rapidly took their clothes off.

He pretended to cum and came back for his weapon when Mary left for the ladies room. He threw out an empty condom in the garbage, along with Kleenexes in case Mary looked inside the bin, and hid the knife under one of the fluffy pillows.

When Mary came back, Jack told her he was ready for round two. Flattered, Mary listened to Jack and laid down on her fragile back like a good girl. They had sex again. This time, Jack had an orgasm and cut Mary's throat while he was still inside her.

Jack rummaged trough the woman's leather purse and found her wallet. He might as well help himself! He found out her name was Nicole Cardinal and laughed out loud at this amusing discovery.

Mary Ann Polly Nichols was Jack the Ripper's first accepted victim according to all his research. In reality, she was actually his third major victim. Jack had used a previously unanimous Nicole Cardinal to portray his third past life victim for his new game, and she turned out to somewhat have the third victim's name within her own. It was coincidentally perfect!

Jack took the time to write a quick note that simply said: J.A.C.K. and left it by the dead green eyed woman. He did not think that anyone would made the connection to Jack the Ripper yet, but in time they would.

Jack left Nicole's apartment with a dark green plastic garbage bag in hand. He didn't want to leave any semen behind! Sex crimes were much more complicated than he remembered.

He realised that he might have left evidence of his person on the woman's bed sheets, so he went back and tossed them in one of the machines of the apartment laundry room. He placed the necessary coins needed to make the washer work into their designated slots, making sure not to leave any partial or full finger marks on them. Once they were all in, he covered his thumb with a Kleenex and pushed the mechanism forward to let the money fall into the machine. Jack turned it on without putting soap in it, and went back to the pub for one last drink.

If anyone had seen him drinking earlier or leave with Nicole it would not matter. He had thrown out his rock and roll wig and his first layer of clothing a few blocks away from Nicole's home and re-entered the pub as a new customer.

# Chapter 6:

Jack did not wait too long before finding a woman named Annie in the phone book and turning her into a corpse.

To be safe, Jack wrote the listed number and walked to a nearby payphone. He dialled the ten digits and asked to speak to the man of the house. The elderly woman on the other end replied that she lived alone. Jack asked if it was Annie and she responded in the affirmative. He was in luck! When she asked who the caller was, he responded: "I am nobody" and hung up. He laughed at his own unplanned joke. His stage name had once been Mr. Nobody in his past life.

On September 8th, he sold the nice old lady by the name of Annie Newman some grapes by pretending to be a door-to-door fruit salesman. She sweetly invited him for a nice cold beverage, which he accepted.

Jack murdered kind Annie in her own kitchen after she was finished eating her tiny purple fruits. Jack cut her throat and mutilated her wrinkled body. He left his new signature note "J.A.C.K" and the words "poor Annie" by the left side of her grey head before heading back home with his leftover bag of fresh grapes.

He knew that authorities would be confused by the age difference between Nicole and Annie, but at least they would not look for a pattern just yet.

Jack still wanted to leave a little clue, even though police might not even find it helpful. He posted a letter addressed to detective Smith, now retired, that simply read: *"Won't it be nice to have the good old times again? J.A.C.K"*

# Chapter 7:

Jack decided to spice things up a little bit by writing a fun note to the press. It read:

*"Dear Boss,*
*I have killed several times before and laughed at everyone for always being on the wrong track. I hope you will all like this new little game. I love my work and can't wait to start again. My knife is nice and sharp. I would like to get to work again soon, but must wait a few days.*
*Yours truly,*
*J.A.C.K"*

The original letter, dated September 25th, was given to the police. A copy had been made beforehand for publishing purposes but it never made it into the next day's paper. The letter was not to be mentioned. Jack was not happy about the lack of publicity he got.

At the end of the month, Jack wrote another letter.

*"I will give you a tip. You will hear all about Jack's double murder soon. I will cut the ears off of one girl and send it to the only person who knows who I am.*
*J.A.C.K"*

The letter was only received on the first of October, the day after Jack had completed his work.

The press was unauthorized to make mention of this letter either, so Jack had to find another way to get attention.

# Chapter 8:

Dr. George Philips received an express package at his rich London home. Inside, one bloody human left ear with a round gold earring attached to it was contained within a large Ziploc bag. A note placed at the bottom of the box read:

"*Dear George,*
*I managed to find the time to cut both ears off this time. Not just the right lobe. I saved one for myself, and thought I would share the other.*
*I would have sent the knife that cut them, but I still need it. Maybe I will send it to you when I retire, if you are not already dead.*
*You can't catch me, but I dare you to try!*
*From hell,*
*J.H*
*P.S. You might remember me if you try and think a little. Ha, ha*"

Seeing the rotting ear was bad enough, but reading the blood-smeared letter was worse. It was Jack the Ripper's style! It had familiar sentences to it.

The doctor wanted to bring the parcel to the authorities so that they may match it to a body and have the bloody print on the top of the page analysed. However, the doctor stood frozen in place. No murder or missing person had been reported lately and the parcel was stamped almost a week ago. Who was playing with him? There was no return address, but the post office stamp indicated that the parcel had come from Montreal, Canada.

Suddenly, Dr. Philips remembered his former patient-Jack Huntington. How could he have forgotten!?! It was because of this boy that he had restarted his personal investigation on Jack the Ripper after he retired.

The fact that the hypnotized boy mentioned leaving clues everywhere made Dr. Philips look for them despite his mocking inner voice. He read all the biographies of each suspect again. He read back the letters and reports he owned, trying to make sense of it all.

Flipping through pictures inserted into the books, he realised how many Jack the Ripper portraits the artist Walter Sickert had done. That in itself was not enough to pin him as the Ripper, but he still found it very odd that the man had entitled one of his paintings "Jack the Ripper's Bedroom" and had several portraits of faces and scenes that looked too close to the Ripper victims and crime scenes to be a coincidence.

For example, Sickert had a drawing of a wide-eyed woman positioned the same way that Mary Ann Nichols had been found. He also drew one of a woman whose left side of the face was somewhat shadowed. It appeared almost mutilated. In another one of his drawings, a female body was lying in a bed with a similar bed frame to the one Mary Kelly was found in. The woman in question is being attacked by a man. In another portrait, there is a torso in the background. Sickert loved boxing so it was always assumed that the naked torso was a representation of a boxer, but upon closer look it looked female. Several of his drawings had mysterious horizontal lines on the woman's necks. There is no reason for them to be there. In a Jack the Ripper frame of mind, they look like cuts.

Of course, Walter Sickert could have just been drawing what was popular. The general public had access to viewings not accepted today, and were told so many details that the artist could have simply used it as inspiration. But, his morbid side kept Dr. Philips eyes open.

From what Dr. Philips could tell of everything Walter had published as well as numerous letters found that had been sent out from him, it became quite obvious that the man loved to write as much as Jack the Ripper did.

Latest evidence showed that most of the Ripper letters had been written with paint or high quality inks only a wealthy man could afford. The artist had debts, but he was not poor. Sure, a lot of the letters suggested that Jack the Ripper was not a rich man, but how could he have obtained such expensive writing material if he was penniless?

Also, Walter had been known to write with chalk on his studio walls just like Jack the Ripper had done in a public area.

The Ripper letters sometimes mentioned horse races, which was something Walter was known to place bets on. This seemed so insignificant before.

Walter Sickert had been an actor as well, so he was trained on how to disguise his traits and voice. He could have easily owned many moustaches and hats, as some of the Ripper letters mentioned, as well as costumes. He could make himself look tall by an exaggerated erect posture or shorter by slumping his back. This could account for the multiple witness descriptions. He would have also known how to give himself another appearance. Walter actually changed his own personal appearance several times in his adult life.

What really intrigued Dr. Philips, was that in one of Sickert's paintings there was an image that almost looked like a bird, maybe a seagull, behind a woman's ear. If you looked at it from a different perspective, the white blob also looked like part of a man's face. People saw what they wanted to see, but many people thought that Walter might have been hinting at his personal opinion that Dr. Gull was Jack the Ripper. It was a bit ridiculous, but what if this was one of Jack the Ripper's twisted hints? An illusion that was barely noticeable, but so obvious once you saw it.

Could it be possible that the doctor had given the medical information the artist lacked, to do a job he could not do himself? Dr. Philips had done extensive research and started believing that the most recent theories about the case made more sense, but felt that it still had holes in it.

What if Dr. Gull and Sickert worked together to hide the Royal Family's dark secret? They most certainly complimented each other! And hadn't Jack written in one of his letters that he had had somebody else mail that letter in question. Several notes were written on the exact same day, but posted from different locations. Some that would have been impossible to be on the same day. Those letters were written from the exact same stationary.

Maybe Jack the Ripper DID murder more women than most people thought. Didn't a lot of Walter Sickert's art students disappear without a trace?

Dr. Philips suddenly regretted letting the boy leave the institution. He wondered if a new partner was found, if there was ever one to begin with. Had it been Dr. Gull? He still made the most sense. Would each modern man fit past life characteristics?

He needed to get a hold of the Canadian police fast, but wasn't sure what he would tell them. Obviously, he would need to tell them about the package, but could not bring the bloody ear with him. He decided to take a picture of his unwanted present along with the box it came in. He even took a picture of the letter that came with it. He would hand in the evidence to the local police, then make an urgent trip to Montreal.

# Chapter 9:

One week ago, Jack found two victims and dumped their bodies within a Jewish district.

Jack specifically asked for escorts named Elizabeth and Catherine. He requested that the ladies present themselves directly at his cheap hotel room at exactly midnight. Of course, he registered under a false name and planned on paying the hourly rate using pure, untraceable cash.

Maybe he was becoming a bit paranoid, but when he took out money from the bank to use as a safe alternative payment from his identification credit cards or Interac, Jack always ended up going to another branch days later to exchange his twenties for tens, and then asked another bank to exchange them back to twenties. No debit cards were requested during these live exchanges so the serial numbers on the money could never be linked to him. Jack did not do this often, but when he did, he used a disguise because of the cameras. He kept all his safe money in an envelope.

When the tall sexy blond girls arrived, Jack let them in his hotel room and gave them red wine with a high dose of crushed sleeping pills. He waited until Elizabeth and Catherine passed out and carried each sleeping body to his car. He could have done his work indoors, but was afraid of being caught putting the mutilated bodies inside his vehicle afterwards. If he was caught now, he could say that the girls had passed out and that he was taking them back to the agency.

His car was parked right in front of his hotel room door, so carrying the girls to his back seat was an easy job. He covered the piled up bodies with a blanket and drove off.

Jack found a secure spot to open the bodies up and take what he wanted. He left a womb-less Elizabeth near a Jewish school, and an earless Catherine in the same school's yard. He tore a piece of her dress and left the bloody fabric in front of the main entrance.

He didn't have anything against Jews, aside from the fact that his birth parents had been Jewish, and could not leave without writing a chalked message behind like he had done in the past. As a teacher, he often pocketed chalk after writing on the blackboard. He took out a piece and wrote on the brick wall that the Jews should not be blamed for nothing.

He left his usual signature note J.A.C.K on both victims.

As an afterthought, he went back to Elizabeth's body and punched her in the mouth to remove all her front teeth. It was the first time he considered making his new victims looks like his past ones.

The announcements and articles about Jack's recent work, which included an earlobe with an attached earring sent to the police station, made Jack the Ripper fanatics provide their insights to the police.

They predicted that another murder would occur on November 9th, and that a woman by the name of Mary would be the victim. That narrowed things down! Police sarcastically thought. J.A.C.K didn't seem to pick out a specific type of victim. He just went by name alone.

The prediction was announced on the news and in the papers, but the police could not protect every single woman named Mary. There were too many! The best thing they could do was put up warning posters around the surrounding neighbourhoods and double their regular surveillance that night.

# Chapter 10:

Dr. Philips opened his front door and saw a dark blue car parked in his driveway. An unfamiliar man got out of the rented vehicle and waked towards him. "Where are you going in such a hurry?" he asked. "I have an important errand to run and I am already late", the doctor responded without taking much interest in the stranger. The man grabbed Dr. Philips arm as he walk by and looked at him straight in the eyes. "It looks like I caught you first, Doctor".

Before the doctor could process what was going on, he felt extreme pain on his left side. Jack forced him back into the castle-like house and told him who he was. "You've always been good to me, but I am afraid that I have no choice but to kill you. Otherwise, you will ruin my fun".

Jack finished what he started and gutted the dead doctor. Afterwards, he hung the man by his own intestines and placed a note inside his open stomach.

Before leaving, Jack took a big bite out of the man's right arm with a set of false teeth. The last dead body he took a bite out of was examined and dental records were pulled out. He wasn't about to make the same mistake again!

Previously, his dentist only had x-rays of the imperfect teeth he had before being given braces. Jack's old dental records were never matched to the bite mark done with his new and improved teeth alignment. He had since then changed dentists and his record was now up to date. Jack didn't care that he was in another country. He took every precaution he could to avoid getting caught.

Jack chewed on the raw piece of meat on his way out the door, and dumped his temporary teeth inside one of the neighbourhood's garbage.

The maid found her employer's body and fainted.

When police arrived, they could barely read the letters J.A.C.K on the bloody paper. However, it was enough for them to make a connection between this brutal murder and the female torso they had found earlier that day. The same note had been found underneath Jack's birth mother.

Since his birth father, Dr. Huntington, had died of lung cancer a year ago, Jack found it easy to enter his former home and hack his abandoning mother to pieces. He had thrown everything, except for her naked torso, in the Thames River before paying his childhood psychologist one last visit.

Jack took the time to buy an oyster card, hop on a tube and stop at the Tower Hill underground station to go on one of the famous Jack the Ripper walks.

It rained the entire time, but Jack did not mind. He followed his female tour guide with an umbrella in hand, and listened as she explained how prostitutes used to stay around churches and go into alleyways with their clients.

His small group was told that Mary Ann Polly Nichols had been found in Old Buck's row, now Durward street, on August 31, 1888. They did not walk there because it would have taken up a good part of the tour. They walked to all the other major crime sites, but not in the order the murders took place.

They first headed towards Burner Street, where Elizabeth Stride's body had been found with her throat cut open the night on September 30th. The tour guide explained how, on the same night, Catherine Eddowes' body had been found about a mile away.

The group ventured towards Mitre Square were Catherine had been found, and did a small detour toward the location her bloody apron had been left with the chalked words above.

Images of how each location looked back in 1888 flashed through Jack's mind as they stopped in front of each one of them. It was still light out, but he could see the dark skies.

They proceeded to walk to Miller's court where Mary Kelly had been mutilated in her home on November 9th. While the group looked towards the reconstructed lodging house, a man on his bicycle unexpectedly passed by and randomly yelled out "Jack the Ripper!", which made a couple of startled women scream and Jack snap back to reality.

The entertaining tour ended where Annie Chapman had been found the night of September 8th.

The Ten Bell pub was nearby, so Jack went inside for a visit like the tour guide recommended. He felt very nostalgic in the old damp pub.

After a few drinks, Jack walked around Whitechapel on his own, remembering his old life.

Jack could almost see the overpopulated streets, all the homeless people who could not afford basic shelter, and all the drunken prostitutes. He could practically smell the sewage that polluted the smoggy air back then, making people hide their mouths and noses to avoid throwing up. He could hear the flies annoyingly buzzing around the stench of the poor neighbourhood, the alley cats and the stray dogs. He could almost hear the imaginary horses feet hitting the ground as they pulled carriages onto the narrow streets, occasionally stepping into puddles of mud. He heard the voices of small children begging for food, and saw them eat rotten vegetables and meat. The East End was a place for the poor or penniless citizens. The rich dared not venture into that part of the city.

It was barely ever sunny in London. It rained on and off constantly. The nights were pitch black and the streets were so poorly lit.

Jack went past a dark alleyway that had a spray painted shadow of a man in a top hat, presumably Jack the Ripper. He was highly amused by that sight. He had many fans, even now, and he liked it.

Jack walked all the way to Polly's murder sight and saw that tall bushes had grown on the past crime scene. Jack had a flashback of Polly's murder, and left the site with a smile on his face.

He took the time to visit all his other Whitechapel murder sites, passing by the previous location of workhouses. Jack even walked by one of his many secret old lodging houses. He remembered being told by the landlady that she knew who Jack the Ripper was, but she had not said HIS name. He couldn't remember who the lady had presumed it was. All he remembered was that she had been so close to the truth, yet so far away from being right.

Jack considered visiting the graves of his most famous victims, but remembered his past life experience with that. He had been high on opium and the woman he had murdered seemed to nag at him from within the cemetery. Although he had given up drugs long ago, Jack was afraid of hearing the angry voices of Mary Ann, Annie, Elizabeth, Catherine or Mary Kelly. Chances were that their souls had been reincarnated like his own, but he feared that some supernatural link could somehow alert the new women of his return. If they still wanted revenge…

His last stop of the night was going back to the place he had left his present life mother's torso. A large double sided sign, not meant to be comical, yet hilarious to Jack, described the crime committed at this very spot and warned people to be on the lookout. Jack had noticed several of these announcements throughout the city. He wondered what Montreal would have looked like during his "just another common kill" days if that city had done the same.

There were so many things that Jack wanted to visit in London.

He was curious about the London dungeon because he saw several advertisements showing that there was a new Jack the Ripper exhibit inside. What interested him the most though, what visiting the art museums to see if he could spot his old paintings, the theatres he once performed in, and the supposedly haunted Tower of London.

Jack recalled part of the latter catching on fire while he was in the city. In fact, he remembered another time were London itself had burned. He was not alive during the great fire of London, but there was a big fire a few years before his killing spree started.

Everything had changed so much! London wasn't as dirty as he remembered. There was smog, but the air was still fresher than it used to be. The Thames looked clean too, although there were probably a lot of bones at the bottom. So many chunks of memories were left behind, yet the city looked like it had been completely rebuilt. You could no longer cross the river by the Tower Bridge underground tunnel. Many bridges had been built over the water.

There were busy underground stations, where large painted letters and an occasional female voice reminded everyone to mind the gap. Jack wanted to find somebody skinny enough to fit between the tube and platform so that he could leave them there to suffer. He imagined many painful accidents, much like those in the Montreal Metro stations.

His thoughts were interrupted by a suicide attempt. Jack found it very inconsiderate of the man to have jumped in front of the train while so many people depended on public transportation. Now he would either have to wait around until the tube ran again, or find another way to get to his hotel. He now regretted leaving his rental car in the parking lot.

Jack would have adored to continue his game where he had originally played it, but he was not familiar enough with the changed Whitechapel neighbourhood. Plus, with all the bombings going on, surveillance was elaborate everywhere. He had no place to clean up and could not walk into his hotel with blood all over himself. He was lucky to have been able to use his former doctor and mother's houses previously.

He was slightly upset at not being able to murder one of the guides doing the Jack the Ripper tours. He had observed that none of the companies required their animators to wear costumes, which had disappointed him. But, he still would have liked to leave a body in Whitechapel, under the graffiti he had adored.

Unfortunately, fulfilling this fantasy was too risky for the same reasons he could not continue playing his original game here. It would have been fun to leave a tour's pamphlet behind as an ironic clue, but he was afraid of getting caught red handed. He would just have to come back some other time.

If he had the chance, he would buy a period dress to leave on the victim. This thought made him wish he had come up with this idea sooner. He wasn't about to change his style now though. Then again, it could confuse the police.

Before leaving his birth country to return to Canada, Jack left a postcard in a mail box with the words: *"Jack is alive. You will have a job to catch me. Ta, ta"* written on it. No postage was paid.

He had used his mother's blood to write the message and had left her bloody fingerprint on it. The front of the card showed an artistic picture of Jack the Ripper. He'd been carrying the non-stamped card with him, inside a Ziploc bag, during the Jack the Ripper tour.

He had also been carrying his birth mother's right eyeball, and his former psychiatrist's left one as souvenirs of his trip. Although he had stopped collecting body parts for himself long ago in exchange for newspaper articles, he felt a need to keep a more concrete part of his past with him.

Jack wanted to put the eyes inside the new souvenir journal he had made to keep all his latest clipping so that his birth mother and former psychologist may see what he had done. He planned on keeping ice packs inside the single Ziploc bag he kept the eyes in to help them stay fresh. This would keep the book open, but he planned on cutting the front of the eyes eventually and sticking them flat into his journal.

# Chapter 11:

Jack returned to Canada to finish his Ripper saga.

He had been observing his former neighbour Mary for quite some time, but she never accepted to go out with him despite his good looks and charm. She always had bogus excuses not to see him, but Jack saw men coming and going from her apartment quite often. He asked her about it one day and she got really upset with him. She told him to stop stalking her or she would file a report against him and sign a restraining order.

Jack had always held a grudge against Mary and knew that he would get back at her one day for never giving him a fair chance. What better time than now that he needed a victim called Mary.

Jack was patient enough to wait until November 9th before butchering Mary. He broke Mary's window in the middle of the night and managed to slip his arm inside to unlock the side door.

He entered the house quietly and heard the sound of a man and a woman moaning loudly. Mary was obviously not alone. Jack decided to hide in a closet and wait to see if the man would be spending the night or leave.

After one hour of hearing them both moan with pleasure, Jack headed towards the garage, grabbed an axe, and ran up the stairs. He opened the bedroom door and hacked the naked man with his new toy. He looked at Mary and brought down the axe on her next. He cut her up so badly that she wasn't even recognisable.

Like Mary Jane Kelly, Jack cut up her face until she had no features left. He cut off her ears and her nose. Part of her skull could be seen on her right side. He hacked up her naked body, destroying her genitals. He surgically removed her breasts and placed them on her bedside table, along with her kidney. Every single organ was removed and thrown somewhere inside the room. There was blood everywhere! Mary's light brown hair was now dark.

The previously white bed sheets were soaked by the time Jack was finished. The liquid dripped onto the carpeted floor.

Jack left his J.A.C.K note in the bedroom on top on the Victorian style dress he originally bought for Mary and made his way to the bathroom to shower. He burned his bloody outfit in the fireplace. He then stole the man's clothes, and left the house wearing them.

Police imagined that this would be the end of J.A.C.K since Jack the Ripper technically only had five well known victims and the copycat seemed to have found a woman to represent each old victim.

No suspects had yet been brought to the station since witnesses were rare and unhelpful.

There was a woman who had managed to survive an attack back in July. She had told police back then that a strange man had rang her doorbell and tried stabbing her in the throat. She struggled and screamed bloody murder, scaring the man away. Police had taken the man's description and were still on the lookout for a short skinny man in his early thirties, with light brown hair and green eyes. The man had a thick curly moustache at the time, but may have shaven it off since the artist sketch was posted in the newspapers.

"Police think there may have been a connection between Mrs. Wilson's attack and Martha's August murder because of the need to go for the throat. Police think that J.A.C.K might have been practicing before choosing his copycat victims, but are still investigating."

Jack read the papers and was glad to see that the police were looking for a man that did not fit his description at all. But, he was insulted that they could think he would leave a survivor without ever going back to finish the job. What kind of guy did they think he was?

He wrote them a letter.

*"Dear fools.*

*You think you're so clever and talk about being on the right track. The police pass me every day, and I shall pass one going to post this. No use trying to catch me.*

*Love, J.A.C.K"*

# Chapter 12:

On the 20<sup>th</sup> of November, Jack drove by a little farmhouse and decided to pay the farmers a visit. He parked his car on the side of the dirt road and walked along the long path towards the front door.

Jack rang the doorbell and waited a few minutes before circling the house.

In the distant field, he could see tractors and other farming machines slowly moving. There were cows too busy chewing their grass to notice him. The donkey however, greeted him with the loudest "hee-han" Jack had ever heard. The excited animal tried to walk away from the tree he was attached to, and sounded his noise non-stop until a woman stepped out of the old barn.

Jack apologized for his intrusion, and told the lady dressed in overall jeans, rain boots, a chequered shirt and a straw hat that his car broke down and needed towing. He asked to use the phone.

The tanned woman walked towards her house and motioned Jack to follow her inside. The place seemed deserted. "It's very quiet in here", Jack commented to verify if they were alone. The woman answered that the men were out working in the field and that the girls were out picking vegetables or helping her in the barn starting at six in the morning. Jack was pleased to know he was safe to kill.

"Mrs. Farmer", he started, "I do apologise again for disturbing you". "That is quite alright", she answered with a southern accent without giving Jack her real name. "People stop here all the time". "I am sure they do" Jack continued. "Thanks for being such a good sport". As he finished those words, Jack took two steps forward, cut the woman's throat and let her fall to the ground.

He left the house and came back with a black top hat, which he had purchased at a costume shop at a discounted price the day after Halloween. He dropped the hat upside down beside the dead woman and left his J.A.C.K note inside of it.

Police brought Ripperologists into the investigation after finding this clue. The dress found at Mary's murder scene had never been made public so police did not believe they were looking for a copycat of the previous murders, even if the handwriting of the new note did not quite match the five other ones. They were all strangely similar, yet different. Since Jack the Ripper letters had been received in different styles of handwritings, the police assumed that the new killer was mimicking his idol's work to the last bit.

After hearing the names of all the recent murder victims, Ripper experts thought that the Jack the Ripper influenced killer might have purposely left the previously attacked Mrs. Wilson alive for her to give a false description of a suspect. Men do not have big moustaches these days, and Ada Wilson had been a possible Jack the Ripper survivor back in 1888, although it was in the month of March, not July.

They pointed out the fact that Emma Smith and Martha Tabram were also possible Jack the Ripper victims and that the dates that Emma Madison the prostitute and Martha Sigma the escort were found matched the dates of the 1888 murders.

They also pointed out that a Mrs. Farmer had been a possible Ripper victim on November 20 of that year, so Jack may have killed a woman farmer to represent the past victim. They suggested that he might have a bad sense of humour.

The Ripperologists inquired if there might have been a woman by the name of Fay found during the month of December, most likely on the 26, about a year ago or an Annie found in February, most likely on the 25, of the following year. No murders matching those names and or dates had been reported, but police searched for missing persons just in case the bodies were yet to be found.

Ripperologists also asked, out of curiosity, if a woman's torso had ever been found during the month of October. The discovery in London, England had not been heard of in Canada.

Ripper experts helped the police come up with the names of possible future victims and estimated murder dates; Rose in December, Elizabeth in June, Alice in July, Lydia in September, Frances in February and Carrie in April. They noted that Frances and Carrie's murders might happen a while after the others, if at all.

While they discussed, Jack wrote another fun message. *"I am Jack the Ripper. Catch me if you can!"* He mixed up a bit of his previous victim's blood with some dark red and brown paints to write his note, and used a paintbrush to write it with. At the very bottom of his page, he drew a stick figure of himself.

# Chapter 13:

Police became much too present for Jack to want to stick around Montreal for his next murder. They were probably expecting him to kill a woman named Rose, so calling an escort agency was not a possibility and asking around for a Rose would elevate suspicion too. He could look in the phone book again, but decided to just leave the city around the time of his murder and try an escort agency farther away.

He did not want to change the date of his murder because that would ruin his plan. He needed to kill on December 20th.

Jack was about to leave for a weekend trip to Toronto. He was sure to find a victim by the name of Rose there. Worst case scenario, he thought, I will just find a random victim and leave a rose behind with my note. This sudden idea made him cancel his hotel reservation and stay in Montreal. It would be more fun this way.

Five days before Christmas, Jack parked his car in the underground parking lot of the shopping centre and waited for a woman to walk by with her hands full of bags. He had to be patient because the parking garage was not always deserted when a possible victim passed by, but Jack packed himself a sandwich, a chocolate bar and a soda to avoid having to leave his post. He even had a bucket with him in case he felt the need to urinate.

Finally, Jack spotted a middle-aged woman with her arms full of shopping bags and beautifully wrapped packages. He stepped out of his vehicle and walked towards her holding a bouquet of flowers he pretended to have just purchased and offered his help. The woman accepted with gratitude and ranted on the fact that her husband had to work late and that she only got the chance to do her Christmas shopping this very evening for her three kids. Jack listened and helped the woman load her car.

After making sure that they were still alone, Jack stabbed her, cut her throat and left her body beside her car. He unwrapped the paper from the flower arrangement, took out a single rose and placed it on her dead body.

Jack had taken the time to attach his famous note to the rose beforehand.

Police were beginning to consider this murder and the farmer woman's death to be unrelated to the original Ripper Saga, and started believing it was a J.A.C.K copycat after all. The dress found in Mary's room could have been her costume. It was her size. The farmer killer didn't have to know about the dress to want to leave a top hat behind. Maybe he was teasing. Continuing what the other killer did not do. Instead of choosing his victims by name, he was being symbolic. Police nicknamed him, "The Symbol Killer."

It looked like whoever this supposedly new killer was, he might not be alone in wanting to somewhat continue the Ripper Saga in his own way. Either that, or he did not just stick to a single victim at a time.

Jack found out that several days before he killed the unknown woman, a six year old girl named Rose went missing.

Her parents opened their front door and saw a bouquet of fresh red roses on their welcome mat. A strange note was attached to it. It read: *"a live Roses"*. The following day, a single long stem rose was left with a note that said: *"My poor grammar was not a mistake. You have two days to figure out my message (a live Roses), or it will no longer be true. From: the one who took your pretty daughter. J.A.C.K"*

The couple brought the second note to the police. They examined it for prints and got a partial print. Each flower shop employee in the area was questioned. They inquired on who had purchased roses in the last two days, but some customers had paid cash for their flowers. Still, police tracked down every man and woman who made a transaction for roses and finger printed them. No match was found. Police went back to each flower shop to see if cashiers remembered the faces of those who had purchased roses using money, but so many customers had gone in and out that it was hard to get any descriptions.

While one team did inquiries, another team tried to decode the message. They read the note a few times thinking it was a clue to the kidnapper's identity. They fingerprinted people who worked around live roses and asked if anyone was leaving their position as a florist or gardener.

Finally, one officer read all the words in different order and came up with the answer: "Roses a live-Rose is alive!" That was good news, but according to the note, this fact would no longer be true in a few hours.

There were no further instructions from the kidnapper, so officers started getting nervous. They would have no choice but to ask the media for their help in spreading the news that Rose was alive to let the kidnapper know that they had figured out his message.

The next day, December 20th, Rose was found dead with wilted black roses on her stomach. A note attached to the lifeless bouquet read *"dead Roses"*. The first officer who read the note automatically saw the real message "Roses dead-Rose is dead" and became furious.

Jack was slightly bothered by this murder. But, just like in the old days, he did nothing to show that he disapproved of killing children. He let the police falsely connect this unexpected murder to his own, and kept up to date on the news reports.

The search for the kidnapper continued, but it led nowhere. Rose was buried without her killer found.

# Chapter 14:

Neither Jack or his mysterious playmate committed any crimes for close to six months.

During the month of June, Jack wondered if the police might expect him to kill a woman by the name of Elizabeth. He wanted to stick to his original plan, but decided to slightly throw the police off their track again. It would be easier for him to find a Mrs. Jackson anyways.

This time, he used the phone book again and acted like he needed to complete a survey for a statistics company he invented. It took five calls to find a Mrs. Jackson who lived by herself. He took note of the phone number as well as the address and drove to her house.

When he saw the thin black haired woman leave her duplex, Jack got out of his car and started following her down the street. Since nobody was around, he quickly killed her, left his note by her side and disappeared.

Jack's follower committed a murder as well.

On the same night, the Symbol Killer murdered a beautiful woman and dressed her up in an elaborate Elizabethan dress and fake jewel crown.

He left her body in the middle of several silver nickels, dimes and quarters with the picture of Queen Elizabeth the second facing upwards. A few brown pennies as well as a couple of loonies and toonies were placed around her as well.

A J.A.C.K note was left behind.

Police became quite confused by the discovery of these two bodies.

The Elizabethan woman was found first, and was said to have been the work of the Symbol Killer.

When the second body was found, it led police to believe that there were most likely two killers leaving J.A.C.K notes behind at the present time. The original Jack the Ripper copycat, and the Symbol Killer.

The second victim's last name matched that of Jack the Ripper's June 1889 victim and could be considered as part of the original saga that may have started in April of last year with Emma Madison even though no notes had been found, or in August of that same year with Nicole Cardinal when the first note was left.

Authorities stared becoming more aware of the way the original J.A.C.K might be thinking. They were now expecting possible victims with the last names Mackenzie, Heart, Coles and Brown. Of course, they still sent out a general warning for woman with the names Alice, Lydia, Frances or Carrie to be on the lookout on specific dates, which frightened a lot of people.

Ripperologists felt the need to add that police should look for possible past victims named Mrs. Millwood rather than just Annie because an Annie Millwood might have been a Ripper victim on February 25th 1888.

They also suggested to possibly search for a girl who might have been found dead dressed up in a fairy costume, instead of a woman named Fay. "Fairy Fay" had been a possible Jack the Ripper Victim on the 26th of December 1887. With the Symbol Killer, anything weird was possible.

No murders in the last two years matched the new profiles.

Police did not feel that the original J.A.C.K would strike at random, although they might be missing something obvious. He seemed to just strike on the nights of the original murders and find victims based on the names of the women the old killer had killed.

Police tried to find out if anyone by the name of Annie or Mrs. Farmer may have been murdered on the same night the Symbol Killer had killed the farmer woman, and if a woman by the name of Rose or Mrs. Mylett might have been killed on the same day the rose murders were discovered. Having found nothing that resembled J.A.C.K`s simple work, they started doubting what murders were done by whom. They considered the possibility that J.A.C.K might have murdered the farmer woman in a desperate attempt to continue his game, even though many women by the name of Annie lived in Montreal.

Since two murders had occurred on the 20th of December, they thought that one of them might have been J.A.C.K`s work, and the other the Symbol Killer's doing.

With two new bodies found kilometres from each other, it was not impossible to have two crazy murderers on the loose. The estimated times of death for both victims were far too close for them to have been killed by the same person.

Police could not figure out how the Symbol Killer chose his victims, just that he always left something behind to symbolize Jack the Ripper's possible murders.

The confusing mystery of the J.A.C.K murders was the number one story on television and in newspapers.

Unlike in 1888, not all the case details were given, but enough was said to scare women into avoiding going out alone at night. Even prostitutes worked in pairs because anybody could be next.

Without knowing what victims were truly murdered by Jack the Ripper, it was hard to say for sure when J.A.C.K would strike. He seemed to be continuing on a path of his own, so maybe he had future victims in mind that Ripperologists might not even consider. At least the police had something to work with.

The Symbol Killer was not as predictable as J.A.C.K, even if he tried to pass himself off as the same person. The nights of his murders could easily be determined now, but not his victims. Police secretly hoped that he would not get inspired by another serial killer once he completed the Ripper murders.

# Chapter 15:

Jack started hating the fact that he had to be so careful now. Last month, he almost gave his students some information that had not been released yet because the J.A.C.K murders were all the gossiping teenagers whispered about.

They wanted his personal opinion on the matter and thought his answers were rather odd. One of the teenaged girls told her parents about the conversation and Jack, or Mr. Rippler as everyone within the school called him, almost got suspended without pay because of the complaint about him.

Mr. Rippler was subjected to a lecture. His conversation had nothing to do with his teaching subject, and his opinion on a murder case should not have been discussed in detail for most of his class.

Despite his tiny obstacle, Jack was not going to stop his game. He needed to find an Alice or a Miss Mackenzie before July 17th.

Luckily for him, there was a former student in his biology class named Alice who also happened to take catch up evening classes with him. He still had the records of all his previous students` personal information so he thought he would pay her a visit. He had never liked her and sensed that she had never liked him either. He never gave her good grades because she slacked off a lot.

Mr. Rippler's job was eased by all the commotion the J.A.C.K headlines caused. Instead of having to stalk Alice, he kidnapped his temporary student a few days earlier than the planned murder date.

After his night class, he asked if any of the students would feel safer getting a ride home and Alice was among the girls who accepted his offer. She disliked Mr. Rippler with a passion, but had no reason to distrust him.

Alice would be the last night student to be dropped off.

Unfortunately for young Alice, her teacher never drove her home. He drove towards the highway and told Alice that he was taking her someplace safe. Alice told him she would rather go home, but Mr. Rippler wouldn't allow it. He took out his knife and threatened to stab her in the leg if she screamed or showed any sign of distress. He changed his mind after a tiny sound came out of her mouth and told her that she would kill her just like J.A.C.K had killed at the others. She obeyed, but cried silently all the way to Mr. Rippler's house.

Before turning onto his street, Mr. Rippler asked Alice to lay low so that nobody would see her.

He parked his car in the single garage, got the girl out of the car and locked her inside one of the cages he had in his basement. He told her that she would need to stay there until an Alice or two were killed. It was for her own good. Alice thought her teacher was crazy, but did not realise that he was going to kill her yet.

Jack promised that he would not be violent with her if she was good, but would need to use his iron head mask on her to avoid having her shouting while he was gone.

He tried to figure out in his head what his story would be when Alice was reported missing. People had seen them together and he was supposed to bring Alice safely home. He should have killed her and pretended to be a witness, but it was too early for the murder. It had to be on the 17th, not the 15th.

He was sure that the police would eventually want to come into his home and search his place. No problem. As far as everyone knew, he lived in a small apartment and did not own any other property in the city. He had brought people to his cottage on several occasions, but it was one hour away and he did not care if anyone investigated the place.

If the police searched his records and saw that he had already committed a violent act, they may look into his files further and find out that he was a homeowner. They would most likely want to search that place as well. If they did, they would find all his weapons and torture devices. He might have to hide them. He would also have to hide his portraits. Then again, there was nothing wrong with collecting weapons and keeping them in safe places. He could admit to being a collector. Drawing disturbing pictures was not a crime. As a former medical student, the human body in many forms was interesting. He could easily convince the police that he had taken up art as a hobby since he was young and still liked to draw and paint from time to time.

They might wonder why he kept a big house as a studio and an apartment for living in, but he was prepared for that question. The house needed too much maintenance, while an apartment was easier to keep clean. He could think better as an artist in an open space, while he felt crowded in an closed up apartment.

His main concern was that he had to hide Alice someplace else until the 17th. He could hide her inside his trunk, but the police might look there; especially if the girl banged on the hood. If they searched the rest of his car too, they might find evidence from the previous crimes he had committed.

Jack considered keeping Alice in his Iron Maiden, but that would torture her prematurely. If she did not survive for two days and was declared dead on a day other than July 17 it would destroy his perfect game. He needed to keep her alive and kill her the exact same way he had killed Alice Mackenzie back in 1889.

He cursed himself for not planning this murder well. He really preferred random killings now, but had to finish what he started. He still had three more victims to find, but they would be much later. Hopefully the police wouldn't be all over the place anymore by then. He liked his fame but this was too close for comfort. Jack was really panicking.

Jack tied Alice up with his chains, blindfolded her, and put her in the trunk of his car. He drove out to a gas station, filled up his car and left. That gave him an idea.

He drove back to his murder house, covered his floor with a tarp, killed Alice, wrapped her up in the bloody tarp and dumped her body in the woods. He wanted nothing to do with her for the time being.

Jack drove to another gas station after driving around for a bit, purposely spilled gasoline all over the ground and dropped a lit match before entering the store. He watched his car go up in flames as he paid for his gas. Police would never find any bloodstains or fibres that may link him to any of the murders now.

He had to figure out if he was going to say he dropped Alice off at home or if she was still in the car with him when he arrived here. Police would never believe that Alice was killed by J.A.C.K, or even the Symbol Killer, tonight. He could say that he dropped her off safe and sound but maybe she went out later. Or, if she was in the car with him, somebody might have taken her. He liked his first story better. It had been too long since the class had ended for his second story to be believable.

Police cars, fire trucks and ambulances arrived at the gas station before it exploded. The male teenage cashier and Jack were questioned.

Mr. Rippler was then brought home in a police car. He was not suspected of anything, but with his car gone, he was offered a ride.

The following evening, the police returned to Mr. Rippler's apartment with questions regarding Alice. Her parents had called her friends and found out that her former teacher gave her a ride home. However, she never made it back. Jack swore that he dropped the girl off at the house she directed him to and drove away once she was at the door. He never thought to stay until she was inside the house.

Police wanted to take a look inside his home. Although Jack could technically refuse since they had no warrant, he wanted to be co-operative. Police briefly searched the apartment and left satisfied that Mr. Rippler was not holding the girl hostage. Jack decided to volunteer some additional information. It was better to be up front about his other properties than have the police discover them later on. Besides, he was having fun with the police now. Adrenaline pumped into his system. However, the police had no interest in visiting the house or the cottage.

Jack went back to the woods for Alice the night of the 16th but could not find her. How could he lose a dead body? He figured that animals might have taken her someplace else and turned her into a buffet. Great! Jack thought. All this stress and no body! He would have to find another Alice. Jack was furious now. Then again, using Alice for this precise set of murders was a bad idea. Maybe it was a good thing that police would never find her body on the 17th.

Desperate for the next day's kill, Jack took out his phone book again. No McKenzies were listed. Looking on a first name basis required more effort, but he found an Alice and drove to the house right away.

At one o'clock the next morning, Jack rang the doorbell repeatedly. A woman answered the door in her nightgown. Jack pushed the door open, cut the sleepy eyed woman's throat and left.

He would have liked to dissect her, but did not want to risk getting caught by possible other household members or guests.

Jack read in the papers that the girl he had murdered was not named Alice. She had just moved to what people considered to be a safe neighbourhood. The former tenant's name was Alice, but the police did not considered this kill as possibly being one of the original J.A.C.K's doing because no notes were left behind. They did not believe it was the Symbol Killer's doing either because there were no props left behind either.

On top of all this, a woman by the name of Alice had been found with her throat cut near an alleyway. There was a bloody butcher's apron beside the body. A J.A.C.K note was on top of it, but the handwriting did not match any of the other J.A.C.K notes. All the notes looked pretty different, but this one was completely off from the others. The letters were neat and straight rather than sloppy and italic.

Police stated that the alley victim could be the work of another copycat or a way to try fooling the police. They could not be sure. They also considered the possibility that the killer might have written his other notes with the hand he didn't usually write with, and this new one with his usual writing hand. The handwriting of all the notes may not have all matched, but people could have a few different styles of their own. Penmanship could change from one hand to the other.

Jack would have liked to take credit for the other killer's work, just for playing his game, but knew that he could never convince himself that he had killed that woman and it bothered him. He clipped the newspaper article about his non-Alice as a reminder to do better.

A third body had been found with its throat cut.

The blond girl's name was not Alice, but she was wearing the famous Alice in Wonderland's light blue dress and white apron with matching knee high socks and flat black shoes. Playing cards were left around her body, but only the ones that had hearts on them. The queen had the words "Off with her head" writing in miniscule letters. Ripperologists thought the Symbol Killer had a very bad sense of humour since the writer of the classical story was once a suspect in the Ripper case.

The following letter was send to the press, but Jack did not write it. Not this year anyways.

*"The police now reckon my work a practical joke, well well Jacky's a very practical joker, ha.ha.ha."*

It was obvious that whoever had written the note had desperately tried to imitate the handwriting of the J.A.C.K note found on top of the bloody apron, which was stupidly put into print once the news of the various handwritings came out. There were hesitation marks and it was clear that the writer had taken his time to do each letter very carefully.

Upon first examination, it was concluded that the letter was not written by the same person who had left the recent J.A.C.K note behind. It did match the exact wording to that of a letter possibly written by Jack the Ripper back in 1888 though.

Because the previously mailed letters had never been released to the public, police eventually declared that J.A.C.K and the Symbol Killer were one and the same. This person was using different types of handwriting, just like the 1888 killer had.

Jack had gotten used to other's mimicking his work and was mostly flattered, but this was too much! He needed to be more original than this new playmate and competitor, who was getting full credit for all of his recent work.

A few weeks later, Jack stopped being jealous of the previously named Symbol Killer. A suspect by the name of Joey Knight was arrested and brought to the police station.

Joey had rented out a girl's Alice costume and never returned it. He claimed that he had rented the costume for a play and had lost his bag somewhere after the show. His story checked out. He was a drama teacher in elementary school and was indeed putting up a production of the Lewis Caroll story.

Some of his alibis for the nights of the other suspected murders were questionable.

Joey's stories had to be investigated, and the fact that an Elizabethan dress, top hat and apron were missing from the school's Drama department was not in his favour.

While Joey was being temporarily locked up, Jack could fully relax because the negative attention was focused on somebody else. His worst fear was getting caught, and he no longer had a problem with his buddy taking the fall for some of his work if it meant that he could continue wandering free.

# Chapter 16:

On September 10th, Damien Jack Rippler made up for his previous sloppy work.

He met a lovely lady named Lydia McIntosh, whom he befriended easily. Since she learned to trust him, she had no problem letting Damien into her home on the night Jack decided to drop by for an unexpected visit.

Jack hacked her up into several pieces, and placed her legs and arms in a strong plastic bag. He put her head in another. Jack crammed his garbage bag of limbs into a large sports equipment bag. The head would not fit, so he stuffed it into a backpack.

Damien Jack Rippler drove as close to the St-Laurence River as he could with his body parts and walked to go dump the sports bag inside the water. He then took the backpack and dropped it farther away.

Lydia's torso was found next to a garbage dump, where a J.A.C.K note was left behind, but the victim could not be identified.

It took weeks for police to make an assumption that the remains may have belonged to a Lydia Klein because she was eventually reported missing by a concerned Damien. But, nobody (aside from Damien Jack Rippler) could say for sure.

Damien Jack Rippler obviously kept his personal thoughts to himself. The only thing Damian Jack Rippler told police was that he and Lydia were supposed to go out one night and she never showed up. He called her several times and she never returned his call so he decided to drive to her house. The lights were on, but nobody answered the door. It was very unusual for Lydia to ignore people, so he knew something was wrong.

The fact that Damien Jack Rippler had been in close contact with two missing females in the last two months brought on suspicion; especially that the two names had previously been identified as being potential victims of J.A.C.K.

Police were still on the lookout for a single Jack the Ripper copycat, and if this new Jack had continued his game, this would most likely be part of it.

The police were no longer amused by Jack's name despite the fact that he had started introducing himself as Damien rather than Jack. They searched records for name changes and reasons. When they saw that Damien Jack Rippler had been forced to change his name from Jack Duff after being a key witness to the Ragner family murders, they stopped looking at his name as a form of personal tease.

However, they did look further into his background and discovered that his adoptive parents had been found dead by him. Although, the autopsy reports from the Duff's came back clean, Damien Jack Rippler was not going to be let go so easily.

He was brought in for more questioning. His bar fight was brought up, along with the body found days later. Police caught on to the fact that Jack had used the same worried story that the woman had used to enter her cocaine addicted boyfriend's house before a body was found. They searched Lydia's house but found nothing.

No solid evidence of Jack's involvement with any of the J.A.C.K deaths could be found, and his handwriting did not match any of the notes or letters so he had to be let go. He was relieved, even if he ended up being fired from his teaching job.

Jack had never been a suspect during his past life, and could not believe how close he came to getting caught again. It was his own fault for reporting Lydia missing. He could have just moved on, but had been afraid that nobody would have realised the woman was missing. Lydia did not seam to have any friends and she had proven not to be social with her neighbours. Jack had doubted that any of them even knew her name.

Damien Jack Rippler later found out that while he was being kept inside the station, another woman was found with her throat cut. Her heart had been taken from her, which made police roll their eyes in disbelief that the Symbol Killer had struck again; Lydia Heart had been one of Jack the Ripper's past victims.

There was finally enough evidence to finally arrest former suspect Joey Knight for the Symbol murders. The Elizabethan dress and apron had never been returned to the school, only the top hat a student had borrowed without signing the usual paperwork. Everyone who had access to the costumes had tight alibis for the nights of the murders in which the missing props had been found.

It turned out that Joey's alibis for some of the murder nights had been false. His friends meant well in wanting to protect him, but when they saw his bloody shirt the same night a woman with no heart had been found, they all came clean. The blood on Joey's shirt was proven to have belonged to the heartless victim.

Mr. Knight would soon be put on trial.

When Jack watched the news regarding this new public excitement, he thought he recognised the face of the suspect. He stared at a mug shot in the newspaper and soon saw that it was his foster brother Jake.

The "kid" had evidently lost a lot of weight since the last time he had seen him. He had grown his brown hair long, but it was definitely him! You could always identify people by their eyes. Jake's were a shade of green he could never forget.

Jack wrote a letter to his former foster brother and sent it to him in jail. *"Little brother, what have you gotten yourself into?"* He did not sign his name, but the now grown man who received the letter knew who had written it.

Joey, formally known as Jake, wrote Jack a letter and asked his lawyer to find him to give him the envelope it was concealed in. *"Dear Walter, I may have had amnesia back then, but I remember everything now. I know who you are. Your adolescent journal helped me discover who I was too. It looks like you didn't need my professional insight this time. You went straight to medical school yourself and took care of things the way you wanted. I wished to be part of your game again, even if there was nothing to hide this time. I wanted to help plant false evidence like we did with the leather apron back in 1888, but it looks like I messed up. I thought that writing notes in the same type of handwriting you had when we lived together would be a good thing. I had practiced so much in case I would need it one day and figured that you would modify it just a little bit every time you wrote a new one. I should have let you play by yourself. But, it had been so much fun before! I enjoyed sending out letters again. I thought I could be like you but I failed. Sorry! Will"*

Unfortunately for Jack, his connection to the caught killer eventually made him a suspect in the original J.A.C.K murders again. Police eventually made the connection to Joey Knight as once being Jake Ragner, and thought that the two reunited men might have worked together to recreate the Ripper saga.

"Jack the Ripper worked completely alone now!" Jack wanted to yell, but remained as calm as he could. Lucky for Jack, no concrete evidence could be found on him. His morbid art and torture devices had been moved to a new home in Vancouver, British Columbia, so his non-apartment home looked as normal as any other person's when it was searched.

Jack had joined a theatre company when he lost his job, so he would have been able to explain all the men costumes and wigs he owned. But, nobody ever asked him about them.

Before Jack's investigation could go any further, Joey confessed to all the J.A.C.K murders. His lawyer had advised him to plead guilty in exchange for a lower jail sentence since he was sure to lose the case.

Joey felt like he no longer had anything to lose, so he ended up confessing to more murders than necessary. He thought he could help Jack by being punished for all the J.A.C.K murders rather than simply taking the fall as the Symbol Killer.

He wrote a confession before going to court. Joey refused to give all the details of the murders, which led many to believe that he did not commit as many murders as he claimed. He was sentenced to 30 years in prison anyways.

The rest of the female body, presumed to be that of Lydia McIntosh, took a while to find. It had dawned on some Ripperologists that if the killer of the unknown body was still being inspired by Jack the Ripper's murders, he might have dumped the rest of the body inside a nearby lake or river. Scuba divers started a search in the St-Laurence.

Only one bag was found. When the crime scene investigators opened the wet bag, they found swamp like liquid inside with bloated limbs floating in it.

# Chapter 17:

Jack started getting bored with his latest game because too many other criminals had written to the papers pretending they were J.A.C.K and committed similar murders to him and his locked up foster brother. Too many women had been found with their throats cut.

Of course, Jack was brought to the police station as a suspect again. Not everyone had accepted Joey as being the original J.A.C.K, just the Symbol Killer. Jack was lucky that murders similar to his own were committed while he was locked up. He was left alone after that.

Even though his game no longer pleased him as much as it had at the beginning, Jack felt a need to find the two last victims he planned on killing nonethe less.

A year and half went by before Jack could continue playing his Jack the Ripper role.

But, he found random victims outside the city in the meantime. During his travels, he sent postcards to the Montreal police after each kill and requested that they send their clever officers in the city he was in. He added that he took great pleasure in giving them his whereabouts. Sometimes he would take the plane and other times he would take the train. But mostly, he would just drive. He kept this information to himself.

He wrote two more letters before beginning his travels.

In the first, he simply wrote: *"I am still at liberty. .. Ha,ha,ha!"*

His second letter read as follows:

> *"Good buy four the present. Do not worry, I will be back to finish my work soon enoff. I would never give up.*
>       *From: The Ripper"*

When Jack was in town, Jack spent his a lot of his evenings at the Montreal Hippodrome, betting on horse races. It was just like old times.

While he was in his seat, Jack found a dirty napkin and wrote down his theories about each horse. He planned to mail it to the police with a picture of a mutilated woman, just like he had done in Whitechapel over one hundred years ago.

Jack also bought tickets to a professional wresting match theatre viewing and sent the entrance stub to the police with the letters J.A.C.K written in the back. A brief drawing of a naked torso was sent along with it.

With the Ripperologists working with the police, they simply took the evidence as proof that J.A.C.K was a Jack the Ripper want-to-be rather than clues to this new killer's personality or actual past whereabouts. They did not feel like the mailed papers added to their investigation, any more than all the other notes and letters they received on a daily basis.

No fingerprints could ever be lifted from any of them, and no traces of saliva could be found on the envelopes the J.A.C.K related mail came in. They had all been moistened shut with water or rubbing alcohol.

When there was a return address on the envelopes, they were made up. Only once did an address lead to a real location. But it was the incomplete address of a twenty floor business building, with numerous workers and customers walking in and out.

A few times the police thought they were lucky because barely noticeable strands of hair were found stuck to the papers by static. They turned out to be those of the victims, or unidentified females.

The forensics team felt like they were wasting their time analyzing all the mail, but had to continue in case J.A.C.K or his followers became careless.

During the fall, Jack placed a note inside a glass bottle and threw it in the river. If somebody found it, they would read about all the undiscovered murders he committed outside the city, and his plan to kill a local woman this coming February.

On February 13th, Jack called an escort agency and requested the services of Frances. Evidently, the J.A.C.K murders had been long forgotten because no questions were asked aside from his name. He gave a false name, as usual, and told them he could be reached at his hotel.

Frances showed up at the same hourly motel Jack had met Catherine and Elizabeth years ago. Jack had a bit of fun with the escort and offered to drive her home. When the two reached his car, he cut her throat and drove away.

He cut out the small article written about the murder in the papers. The title read: Is J.A.C.K back to finish his job?

Jack wrote to the Gazette and asked if he had been missed. He also added that he had told Frances that he was Jack the Ripper and had taken his hat off after greeting her. He signed the letter, a friend.

The handwriting matched that of several J.A.C.K letters.

# Chapter 18:

On April 24th, Jack contacted another escort agency and asked for Carrie. She was unavailable, so he called another agency. She was unavailable as well. Every place he contacted had no Carrie's available.

Jack wondered if people had actually remembered his game and started taking it seriously again (better late than never!), of if it was just a coincidence. No matter, he though; he would find a Carrie or a Mrs. Brown before the end of the day.

Finally, Jack picked up a random hooker off the streets and brought her home. He did his business and took her back to an alley where he slit her throat and left the following message in her hand. *"She told me I could call her whatever I wanted, so I screamed out Carrie all night. J.A.C.K."*

He used his right hand to write this note, just to confuse the police again. All his other J.A.C.K notes were written with his left hand. He had tried to create new personal fonts every time, but a few of them looked similar to each other. His "just another common kill" notes had all been written with his right. He was ambidextrous so had no problem writing with either hand, but generally preferred to use the left hand.

# Chapter 19:

In the state of California, a serial killer on death row by the name of Thomas Jackson waited to be executed. The prisoner was asked if he had any last words to say. He yelled out "I am Just another common killer, also known as J.A.C.K!"

As Jack was vacationing in L.A. for the holidays, he saw the man's last words in the papers the following morning. The story about the revelation made it in the evening news.

Although impressed that this man had made the connection between his two major signatures, he was infuriated by the character's audacity in trying to take credit for his fine work. Jack found one last victim and left his last note behind.

*"You never caught me and you never will. Ha,ha*
*Kisses, Just. Another. Common. Killer"*

As far as the world was concerned, Jack completely disappeared afterwards. But the Mr. Hyde in him had never left. In fact, it had become dominant over his nicer personality and he continued to kill whenever he could.

Decades after his killing streak, people still debated who his victims were and were not, which notes were his or from copycats, who he might have been and what his background was. But, since nobody ever caught him, his true identity might never be known.

They might eventually figure out the two last clues he left behind.

His name was changed to John-Aaron Carl Kaminsy shortly after he was diagnosed with generalized cancer. He was eighty one years old by that point. Using names of Jack the Ripper suspects unrelated to who he had really been in the past to form his new full name was his way of telling the world that his new person had a bit of every Ripper suspect in him. His new initials J.A.C.K would die with him.

He did not care about being figured out anymore. In fact, he almost hoped that he would get full credit for his new set of work. Maybe he would see his head in a jar of formaldehyde in one of those criminal museums in another life. He knew that he could not give himself away because he would not be believed and it would take half the fun away. So, he did something obvious that may or may not connect him with his other murders.

Knowing he only had a maximum of two months left to live, Jack found the energy to murder another prostitute by poisoning her and cutting her throat. He left her dead body right in front of his house. Curlers had been placed in her hair to represent Emily Dimmock, and a blanket was placed on top of her naked body.

After his last murder, Jack painted a portrait of his new room and signed it J.A.C.K.

That same summer night, he killed himself by cutting open his own throat. In case he was not figured out on time or at all to be placed among the other serial killers, he placed his will by his side. It indicated that he was a body donor, and wished for his flesh and/or organs to be plasticized and used for science and/or corpse expositions. He would live on, one way or another.

# Sources:

Cornwell, Patricia, «Portrait of a Killer», Cornwell interprises, United states, 2002

Jack the Ripper, published by Pitkin guides (an imprint of Jarrold Publishing) in the UK. No copywrite date listed.

Memories of the Jack the Ripper walk and Whitechapel murder representations at the London dungeon.

Various bits of internet websites discovered from Google searches.
Most popular: www.casebook.org